Welcome to the www.blinddatebrides.com member profile of:
Englishcrumpet (aka Grace Marlowe)

My ideal partner…

Young at heart, just like I am. No cardigan-wearers, please! My teenage daughter has just flown the nest and it's high time I remembered what it's like to be young, free and single. I'd be lying if I said I was looking for a soul mate—true love like that only happens once in a lifetime, and I've been there, done that, worn the black veil…. But I'm looking for someone to share my life with. Preferably someone who loves rock music and cold Chinese takeaway!

My details…

- **Age:** thirty-ten (think about it!)
- **I live:** in London
- **Marital status:** widow
- **Hobbies:** growing old disgracefully

You'll match if you…

- Are young at heart
- Are London-based
- Are unattached
- Want to join me

Read the rest of Englishcrumpet's profile *here*
www.blinddatebrides.com

The Web site www.blinddatebrides.com is running 25 chat rooms and 248 private IM conferences, and 15,472 members are online. Chat with your dating prospects now!

Private IM chat between Kangagirl, Sanfrandani and Englishcrumpet:

Kangagirl:
How was your date?

Sanfrandani:
Weren't you even just a little compatible?

Englishcrumpet:
Erm...there might have been a little kiss...

Kangagirl:
!!!!!!!!!!!

Sanfrandani:
And you turned down a second date? Why?

Englishcrumpet:
He was too "grown-up" for me. And there was way too much chemistry.

Kangagirl:
And that's a bad thing?

Englishcrumpet:
I can't risk falling hard and then losing the man I love again. Surely I'm too old for all that Romeo and Juliet stuff. That kind of all-consuming passion only afflicts teenagers. Doesn't it?

FIONA HARPER
Blind-Date Baby

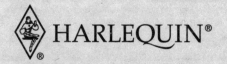

TORONTO • NEW YORK • LONDON
AMSTERDAM • PARIS • SYDNEY • HAMBURG
STOCKHOLM • ATHENS • TOKYO • MILAN • MADRID
PRAGUE • WARSAW • BUDAPEST • AUCKLAND

Recycling programs
for this product may
not exist in your area.

ISBN-13: 978-0-373-18442-2
ISBN-10:   0-373-18442-5

BLIND-DATE BABY

First North American Publication 2009.

Copyright © 2009 by Fiona Harper.

Introducing a brand-new, exciting trilogy
from Harlequin Romance®!

BLIND-DATE BRIDES.com

From first date to wedding date!

Meet three very different women from around the world,
and follow their stories as they find friendship,
love and their happily ever afters with a little help
from the world of online dating!

April 2009
Nine-to-Five Bride **by Jennie Adams**
Meet Kangagirl from Sydney, Australia,
aka Marissa Warren.
She's turning thirty and looking for
Mr. Nice and Ordinary!

May 2009
Blind-Date Baby **by Fiona Harper**
Meet Englishcrumpet from London, England,
aka Grace Marlowe.
Her teenage daughter has left home, and
Grace is looking for a second chance at love!

June 2009
Dream Date with the Millionaire
by Melissa McClone
Meet Sanfrandani from San Francisco, America,
aka Dani Bennett.
She's a career girl who doesn't have time for love—
or so she thinks!

**Three women, three countries,
three exciting love stories.**
Watch it all unfold @ www.blinddatebrides.com.

To my editor, Kimberley Young,
who urged me to dig deeper—
somewhere else—and I found unexpected treasure.

And to Jennie Adams and Melissa McClone—
even the (very) early morning IM chats were a blast!

Don't miss Fiona Harper's
next Harlequin Romance® novel,

Invitation to the Boss's Ball

Available in September

CHAPTER ONE

GRACE MARLOWE and six o'clock in the morning weren't normally on speaking terms. But here she was, standing in the middle of her darkened kitchen, the clock ticking in time with her heartbeat. Pearly light seeped between the slats of the blind, draining all colour from her funky little kitchen. She wrinkled her nose. Everything was grey, even the lime green mugs and the pink toaster. This truly was a repulsive time of day.

What was she doing here? Right about now she should be mumbling incoherently in her sleep, her left foot tucked over the top of the duvet to keep it nice and cool.

In a sudden flurry of movement she turned and headed towards a cupboard—any cupboard—and opened the door. It didn't matter which one. She just needed to be doing something. Because she refused to think about why her little flat seemed like a gaping black hole this morning.

Bags of dried pasta and tins of tomato soup stared

blankly at her from inside the cupboard. She shut the door carefully and tried the next one. Five boxes of breakfast cereal sat in a row, waiting for her to choose one of them. She closed that door too.

The kettle was within easy reach and she absent-mindedly flicked the switch. It roared into life, un-naturally loud in the pre-dawn stillness. She really must get around to de-scaling it some time soon. It boiled so violently when limescale had furred up the insides. The curse of London hard water…

Grace blinked. Just for a few seconds she'd for-gotten to be miserable and lonely. That was good, wasn't it?

She reached for her favourite mug, the oversized baby-pink one with the words 'Hot Mama' spelled out in crimson glitter. A present from Daisy last Mother's Day. Daisy shared Grace's love of kitsch and had known her 'hot mama' would appreciate the sentiment of the slogan and the garish colours.

Daisy had given the mug to her with a twinkle in her eye that had made Grace chuckle, pleased to see proof that her daughter had inherited her sarcastic genes. But when the laughter had subsided, she'd mourned. No more pigtails and scraped knees. Daisy was all grown up and ready to fly the nest.

In fact, she'd already flown.

It was Mother's Day again in a couple of weeks and, for the first time ever, she wouldn't spend it doing something totally fabulous with Daisy. Last year they'd gone to the ice rink and had spent the whole afternoon falling on their bottoms. Then they'd eaten a Chinese takeaway so huge it had gone down in family history as 'the one that could never be surpassed'. But this year Daisy would be in Paris or Romania or Prague. She was going to be away for a whole year. And after backpacking there was university…

Grace hugged the mug to her chest. She missed her daughter already and she'd only been gone eighteen hours. How completely pathetic.

She dropped the mug to the counter with a clunk and stood there, her arms folded and her brows pinched together. Come on, Grace! You're supposed to be the cool one, remember? The mum that all Daisy's friends wished was theirs. The mum who had once worn fishnets and thigh-high boots to parents' evening. The mum who had dressed up as Santa, complete with beard and pot-belly, when little Joseph Stevenson's dad had been too hungover to play the role. The fact that it had been Grace's tequila that had caused the hangover in the first place was neither here nor there…

But Grace didn't feel cool. For the first time in nineteen years she felt old and lonely. And not just wandering-round-not-knowing-what-to-do lonely. There was an ache deep inside her that could only have been caused by someone sneaking into the flat in the middle of the night, carving a huge chunk off her soul and stealing it away. She had a funny feeling that chunk might currently be sleeping in a youth hostel in Montmartre, but she couldn't be entirely sure.

She made the tea and forced herself to turn the light under the cooker hood on. Sitting here in the dark would only give the impression that she was depressed, she thought as she slumped into a chair and lay her head on the table. Steam curled from the mug in front of her and she watched it rise gracefully on unseen currents and drift away. Eventually, she peeled her face from the table top and reached for the mug to take a sip.

Yuck! She stuck the tip of her tongue between her lips and grimaced. What the heck was wrong with her tea this morning? Looking into the mug gave her a pretty big clue. No teabag. Lukewarm water with milk in it was really not her thing.

Sighing, she hauled herself up from the table and crossed to the cupboard where the teabags lived. She reached inside and pulled out the Earl Grey. As she did so, a small pink envelope fell out of the cupboard and fluttered onto the floor.

Teabags forgotten, she bent to retrieve it and stood for a long moment looking at the familiar rounded scrawl that simply read 'Mum'. She smiled. Ever since she'd been able to write, Daisy had had a habit of making her cards and notes, leaving them in unexpected places. Over the years the indecipherable crayon drawings had been gradually replaced by scribbled messages in a neat, even hand, but the flush of joy Grace felt at seeing each one had remained the same. She greedily tore open the envelope and began to read.

Dear Mum,
Please, please, please don't be angry with me for this…

Grace frowned. She knew it! Daisy had borrowed her favourite David Bowie T-shirt last week, and she'd warned her daughter not to get any thoughts about 'accidentally' packing it in her rucksack. Little rascal. A smile turned up one corner of her mouth and she carried on reading.

…but I've got you a little going-away present. I know how much you sacrificed to bring me up on your own, and now it's time for you to have some fun.

Grace stopped reading. A burning sensation tickled her nose and the backs of her eyes. She took another sip of hot water, shuddered and pulled herself together.

No one could have asked for a better daughter. And, somehow, Grace felt that God had blessed her with Daisy to make up for Rob being snatched away from her after such a short time together. Killed by a landmine on active duty in Iraq at the age of twenty-three. Where was the justice in that? He hadn't even lived to see Daisy take her first steps or hear her say 'Dadda'.

Grace sucked in a breath, overcome by the sudden urge to cry, but she shook her head, refusing to give in. She had Daisy. She had to focus on Daisy. Because Daisy had been the reason the sun had kept rising and setting for the last eighteen years.

She looked round the kitchen. Although she knew it was stupid to think so, it was easy to imagine the sun just wouldn't bother to put in an appearance today.

Come on, Grace! Stop wallowing!

She looked again at the letter in her hands. Daisy didn't have to thank her for everything she'd done. It had been her job and her joy. Being a widow at twenty-two had been hard, yes, but every time she looked into those beautiful brown eyes she'd known a big piece of Rob had lived on.

But I know you, Mum. I know you'll talk about moving on or getting a hobby, or finally buying your own coffee shop so you can boss everyone else around instead of being bossed...I also know you'll do absolutely nothing about it. So I've taken the liberty of giving you a little nudge and I make no apologies for

*what I've done. You need this, Mum. Don't you
dare try and wriggle out of it!*

Grace's colourful language as she read the rest of
the letter shattered the greyness of the pre-dawn
kitchen once and for all.

'She did *what*?'

She stared in disbelief at the pink sheets clutched
in her hands. 'You did *what*?' she yelled in the direction of Daisy's bedroom, even though her
daughter had had the good sense to put a few
hundred miles and a large body of water between
them before she'd dropped the bombshell. Very
good thinking. Because, right at this moment, Daisy
would have been lucky to see another sunrise if
she'd been within strangling distance.

Grace stared at the letter once again, then threw
it down on the kitchen table. Despite what Daisy
said, there had to be some way to get out of this.

Noah padded across the cream rug in his study,
absent-mindedly rubbing his damp spiky hair with
a towel. Even though he had already had his
morning run it was still dark outside. And quiet. But
he didn't mind quiet. This was his favourite time of
day. The time where ideas could brew and grow and
take shape.

He turned his computer on. While he'd been
running he'd worked out how to make the villain

of his current novel even more dastardly. His editor would be pleased. The latest in his series of psychological spy thrillers was doing so well, the publishers were pushing to have the next one in as soon as possible.

He carefully folded the towel and hung it over the back of a chair before sitting at his desk and checking his emails. His inbox rapidly filled but, instead of clicking on the top message, he took a little detour, clicking an email link and arriving at a web page he was very careful not to visit when his PA was around. He logged into the site and opened up a page he had marked as a 'favourite' last Monday.

Grace hit the switch in Daisy's room and blinked and squinted in the harsh yellow light. Maybe purple hadn't been the way to go with the colour scheme. It was giving her a headache.

Daisy's baby-pink laptop was on the desk and Grace picked it up and sat on the bed, one foot hooked underneath the other thigh, and settled the machine in the triangle of her legs. The ancient laptop chugged and whirred when she pressed the power button. While she waited for it to boot up, Grace inspected her fingernails and resisted the temptation to pick off some of the electric blue polish. Finally, she opened the web browser and typed in the address Daisy had printed carefully in the PS of her letter.

Blinddatebrides.com! What *had* her daughter been thinking? The thought of going on a date, blind or otherwise, was bad enough—but marriage? Been there, done that, worn the black veil…

A companionable coffee or dinner would be okay. She could probably live through that. While the page loaded, Grace's mind wandered. Blind-date brides? How did that work? You turned up at the restaurant and…what?

Random images stampeded through her mind—wedding dresses made out of co-ordinating table-cloth linen…gold rings as napkin holders…waiters who were really undercover ministers, waiting to pounce at any hint of an 'I do'…

Goose pimples broke out on her legs and worked their way up her body until the fine hairs on her arms raised. She shook her head. Okay, Daisy had undeniably inherited her impulsive genes, but even she wouldn't subject her own mother to that kind of humiliation. Not unless she was present and in the possession of a video camera.

She winced as she typed in the username Daisy had invented to create an account. Frankly, it just added insult to injury. *Englishcrumpet?* Classy. Hadn't Daisy seen enough old *Carry On…* films to know that *crumpet* would attract all the wrong sorts of guys? The sort who always seemed slightly sweaty and tried to peer down your cleavage when they thought you weren't looking. Grace practically had to force her fingers to punch it out on the keyboard.

She logged on to the site and headed straight for the customer service section, bypassing minimalist cartoons of hearts, confetti and kissing stick figures. There had to be a number she could call and yell at someone about identity theft and being made to go on dates you really didn't want to go on. It all looked deceptively easy. She clicked on a friendly-looking button that said 'Contact us'.

Great. 'Customer service teams are available to help you from nine a.m. to six p.m., Monday to Friday,' she read aloud. 'What good is that at—' she checked the display on Daisy's alarm clock '—six twenty-five on a Saturday morning? Most normal people go on dates at the weekend! Fat lot of good you are!' she said to the smiley-face cartoon on the web page, obviously designed to calm and reassure distressed customers. All it made Grace want to do was frisbee the stupid laptop across the room.

Then she spotted another button: 'Email us'.

She stopped scowling and rubbed her finger across the mouse pad to click on the link. Email would work. Not as direct as yelling, but she could use lots of capitals instead. A new window popped up: 'Thank you for spending time letting us know how we can make Blinddatebrides.com better. A customer service representative will respond to your message within twenty-four hours…'

But the date was in less than fourteen hours! Grace was sorely tempted to revisit the whole 'frisbee' idea.

It was far too early in the day to start reading any kind of small print they might have stashed away in the deep recesses of this website. She needed help. Now. She dragged the mouse pointer to a sidebar button that read: 'Chatrooms,' spied a chat headed up 'New to Blinddatebrides.com' and typed, *'HELP!'* Might as well not beat about the bush.

For an instant, her little plea for salvation blinked alone on the page. It was six-thirty in the morning, for goodness' sake! Who in their right mind was going to be trawling for dates at this time of day? Only the utterly desperate—which summed her up quite nicely at the moment, actually.

Then a miracle happened.

Sanfrandani: What's up?

Grace looked around the room. Was this person talking—erm, typing—to her? There was only one thing for it. Grace flexed her fingers and began to type.

Englishcrumpet: I'm new to this.
Kangagirl: Hi, Englishcrumpet! Don't worry, we're all new in this chatroom! How can we help?

Englishcrumpet: Oh! There's two of you! Are you up at the crack of dawn panicking about a date too?

Sanfrandani: LOL! It's almost my bedtime! The 'Sanfran' in Sanfrandani stands for San Francisco.

Kangagirl: And I'm just about to head home from work here in Sydney.

Englishcrumpet: Australia?!

Kangagirl: That's right! Didn't you know this was a global site when you signed up?

Englishcrumpet: I didn't know anything about this site until fifteen minutes ago! That's the problem. Someone else joined on my behalf.

Sanfrandani: How are you finding the site so far?

Englishcrumpet: Well, I found two kind souls willing to help a sister in need, so it can't be all bad.

Grace scratched the tip of her chin with a fingernail. She'd jumped to one conclusion already. Might as well make sure she had her facts straight before she carried on.

Englishcrumpet: You are a girl, right, Sanfrandani?

Sanfrandani: Yes! Believe me, if you saw me, you'd know I was a girl.

In through the nose, out through the mouth…
Grace took a deep breath and dived right in.

*Englishcrumpet: I just found out I have a date
with someone from this site tonight!*
Kangagirl: Good on you, girl!
*Englishcrumpet: But I don't want to go on a
date! I want to know how to get out of it!*
Sanfrandani: Do you have his email address?
Englishcrumpet: No.
*Kangagirl: What about his username? Then
you could contact him through his profile
page.*
Englishcrumpet: I don't know that either!
Sanfrandani: Okay, Crumpet, what do *you
know?*

Grace didn't need the pink page from Daisy's
letter to relay the next bit of information. Every
time she closed her eyes, the words floated in front
of her face. She dropped her lids right then and—
hey presto!

*Englishcrumpet: The note says: Barruci's,
Vinehurst High Street. 8 o'clock.*
Kangagirl: Nice place?
*Englishcrumpet: Erm…I think so. A bit out of
my league. I tend to prefer the Hong Kong
Garden takeaway if I'm spoiling myself.*

Kangagirl: LOL!

Sanfrandani: Why don't you want to go on a date with this guy? The matching system at this site is supposed to be really good. He might just be your type.

Englishcrumpet: Have your dates been perfect matches so far?

Kangagirl: Not bad. On paper they should have been perfect, but just no…you know…

Sanfrandani: So why not go?

Grace's shoulders sagged. There were a million and five reasons why she should stay in, watch bad Saturday night TV and treat herself to a takeaway—especially now she'd mentioned it and was craving roast pork chow mein. What she wouldn't do for a leftover tub of it cold from the fridge right now.

She wasn't going to go. No matter how perfect *on paper* her mystery date might be. It had been years since she'd been on a first date. Of course, after Rob had died, she hadn't even been able to conceive loving anyone else for quite a few years—and she'd had Daisy to bring up. Looking after a toddler on your own was pretty time-consuming.

And later, when she'd thought about dating again…well, a widow just had too much baggage for men her age. It had been a relief when she'd decided to give up trying. None of them had even started to measure up to Rob, anyway. Love like that only happened once in a lifetime.

There was an insistent ping from the laptop.

Kangagirl: Crumpet? Are you still there?
Englishcrumpet: Yes. I'm here.
Sanfrandani: So why not give this guy a try? You can come back tomorrow and share all the gossip with us!
Englishcrumpet: I don't really want to go out with anyone at the moment. I'm a widow.

There was a pause for a few seconds. The usual reaction. People didn't know how to handle it when she told them. Grace sat back, propping herself against the pillows, and waited for the inevitable hasty retreat. These girls would politely excuse themselves and find someone more fun to chat with.

Kangagirl: I'm so sorry, Crumpet. Hugs.
Sanfrandani: Me too. Even if you don't go on the date, come back tomorrow and chat, okay? It's going to take time.

Okay. Now she felt like a real heel. These were perfectly nice women and she was making it sound as if it was all recent history. Had she really been alone that long? She looked round the purple room. Last time she'd been on a first date, there had been teddies on the bed and pony posters on the walls. Now there were shaggy cushions and one of the walls was covered in wallpaper that boasted stylised purple flowers on a silver background.

Englishcrumpet: Actually, my husband died quite some time ago. But what I said is true. I don't really want to go on a date, but I can't leave the poor man sitting there on his own—that would be too cruel. Oh, I'm going to kill my daughter for this when she returns from backpacking!

Kangagirl: Your daughter set you up?!

Sanfrandani: LOL! What's her taste in men like?

Englishcrumpet: Her taste in men is fine—for a nineteen-year-old. I'm just not sure what sort of man she'd choose for her mother!

Kangagirl: I think you should go. He could be cute!

Sanfrandani: What's the worst that could happen? You have a nice meal, chat a little. In a couple of hours it'll all be over and you never have to see him again if you don't want to. At least you'd have got back out there. Next time you could pick someone for yourself. Think about it.

Grace slid the laptop off her legs and left it on the duvet. Her right foot was all tingly from having been sat on for so long and she gave it a shake and stood up to get the blood moving again. Daisy's dressing table stood a few feet away and she walked over to skim her fingertips over the curled edges of one of the photographs tucked into the rim of the mirror.

Daisy smiled back at her, her long dark hair ruffled by the wind, her eyes bright with mischief and easy confidence. Her gaze left the photograph and wandered until she met her own eyes in the mirror and she started. People said that she and Daisy looked more like sisters, rather than mother and daughter, but Grace could always see so much of Rob in her daughter. Just for a moment she was stunned by the similarity between her own reflection and the photograph. Apart from the eye colour, it was as if she were looking at herself in a time warp.

Yes, there were fine lines and wrinkles round her eyes now, and her once slender build had more curves, but she still looked closer to thirty than forty. What a pity that inside her head she was closer to being twenty-one. Being Daisy's buddy had kept her thinking and feeling like that.

What would happen now Daisy was gone—only due to pop in and out of her life in between travels and university courses? Would she turn grey overnight? And it wasn't just her hair she was worried about. She could imagine her skin taking on a dull grey pallor, her eyes becoming glassy. Would she wake up one day and discover an overwhelming urge to wear baggy home-knitted cardigans?

Come on, Grace! Snap out of it.

She twisted to check out her rear end and fluffed her hair with her fingers. She smiled. Even through the striped cotton of her pyjama bottoms, she could tell her derrière could stop traffic in the right pair of jeans. She was way too young to hide it beneath baggy cardigans. She did a little wiggle, just to prove herself right. Her reflection enjoyed the joke and laughed along with her.

See? She was still the same old game-for-anything Grace.

She picked the photograph of Daisy out of the mirror frame and studied it closely. One corner of her mouth lifted. That child was a chip off the old block, no doubt about it. This stunt with the dating agency was just the sort of crazy thing she would have pulled at nineteen. Why was she getting in such a lather about one silly date?

You never have to see him again if you don't want to.

It was time she saw a little more sparkle in her own baby-blues.

She jumped back onto the bed, grabbed the laptop and typed in a frenzy, before she could change her mind.

Englishcrumpet: Okay, girls. I'll do it. I'm going on the date.

After making a quick character sketch for his Ukrainian villain and jotting down some related plot ideas, Noah checked his emails again. He'd better get a move on, though. His PA would be here in twenty minutes and he really ought to finish getting dressed.

Yes, it was Saturday, but he had a big crime writers' conference coming up soon in New York and they needed to go through the final travel arrangements and double-check that the notes for his seminar were all ready to go. Last job would be to proofread his keynote speech for the opening luncheon.

He shook his head, hardly able to believe that this was how his life had turned out.

It seemed he was always travelling, always speaking here and there. Everybody wanted to know what the secret of his success was, as if there were some ingredient other than a modicum of talent and pure hard graft. Living the life of a best-selling author had its great points, but there was a downside he hadn't expected. For a start, he spent far too much time on publicity and promotion and struggled to find time to scribble more than a few words some days. Just as well his army background had taught him discipline and how to be cool under pressure.

And then there were the women.

His friend Harry thought he was crackers to complain about the women, moaning that he'd settle for just one per cent of the female attention Noah seemed to generate.

Oh, Noah had certainly enjoyed glamorous women making a beeline for him in the early days, when his books had first reached the top of the charts. The women had laughed and smiled and hung on his every word, marvelling at how clever and handsome he was and how he was just like a hero in one of his own novels. But after five years it was definitely getting a little tired. He was starting to feel like that guy in the movie who woke up and discovered the previous day was repeating itself. Only, in Noah's case, it seemed to be the previous cocktail party repeating itself.

Okay, the colour of the skimpy dresses and the hair extensions changed. But that was as far as it went. He'd even stopped being surprised how so many stick-thin women professed to love martial arts or were totally fascinated by the cold war. One woman had even spent an hour telling him in great detail exactly how she could strip down an AK47, a hungry glint in her eyes the whole time.

After all his experiences, he could really write a convincing portrait of a glamour vixen who'd do anything to bag herself a rich and successful husband so she could bask in his glory and ride the celebrity merry-go-round for ever. Maybe he'd put such a character in his next book. And maybe he'd have the merry-go-round explode…

Compatibility started with sharing some interests, but it had to go deeper than that, surely. And it had to be a genuine interest, not facts and figures cribbed up on before a date. That was why his new pet project had come in handy. He'd read an article about this website in a Sunday magazine and had been intrigued with the possibility of being able to remain almost anonymous.

He flipped back onto the web page he'd minimised earlier.

Blinddatebrides.com.

If Martine, his PA, knew he'd been surfing on such a site, she'd have fainted.

But what was so surprising about him wanting to find a wife? He was of marriageable age, financially very secure and he had a huge house all to himself. It was just crying out for a wife. And he was fed up going everywhere on his own, being the odd one out at friends' parties, always having to duck into the bathroom to avoid the glamour vixens at the writing 'do's'. Securing a wife would have the added bonus of being the ultimate deterrent.

He wasn't asking for the moon. At forty-one, he was old enough not to fall for all that love-at-first-sight, finding-your-soulmate nonsense. He didn't believe that his soul had another half floating around somewhere, desperately looking to re-attach itself. That sounded like a gruesome scene from one of his novels rather than romantic, anyway.

What he needed was a partner in life. Writing could be a lonely business. He spent days on end on his own, not speaking to anyone, travelling alone. It would be nice to have someone other than a part-time PA in the house. Someone to share a meal and glass of wine with at the end of the day. Someone to bounce ideas off or moan to about the latest deadline. And, if there was a little chemistry there, so much the better.

He'd been on three dates with Blinddatebrides.com so far and all had been unmitigated disasters. The women had been nice in their own way, he supposed, just not suitable at all. He was on the verge of downgrading his expectations in the short-term and just looking for a date-buddy, someone who wouldn't mind attending functions with him to keep the vixens at bay. Even the stupid computer at Blinddatebrides.com—or the trained hamsters, or whatever they used to match people up—should be able to cope with something as simple as that.

Although the match suggestions from Blinddatebrides.com had seemed fine when he'd checked out the profiles, when he'd met the women in person…well, that was where it had all gone wrong.

Hopefully, tonight's choice would buck the trend.

He leaned forward to focus on the pixelated little picture on her profile. Local businesswoman. Age forty. And the picture was intriguing. Dark glossy hair. Stunning blue eyes and the smallest of smiles that hinted at both intelligence and mischief. Not his usual sort, but he'd kept coming back to this profile even after he'd discounted it. And if there was one thing he'd learned from all these years accessing his creative right brain, it was that sometimes you had to ignore the facts and go with your gut.

'Coo-ee!' Martine's voice echoed round his empty kitchen. She'd obviously just let herself in. He reached for the mouse and had just closed the window as she walked through the study door.

'What was that?' she said, eyes fixed on the monitor.

He'd hired her for her razor-sharp instincts, but sometimes he wished he owned a remote control so he could switch them off.

'Nothing for you to poke your nose about in,' he said with a grin and handed her a stack of travel documents.

CHAPTER TWO

THE girl standing behind the reservations desk glanced up at him. It was the same girl as last week. He remembered the neat little bun she wore at the nape of her neck and how he'd wondered if it hurt to scrape one's hair into something that tight. Just like last week, she didn't seem to be in a particularly good mood. A raised eyebrow was all the welcome he got. Good. His attempt at going incognito was working.

'Smith,' he said, returning her look. 'Table for two. Eight o'clock.'

She blinked, then deigned to check the reservations book. 'This way, sir.'

She took off at a brisk pace.

'Has my…dinner companion…arrived yet?'

The girl didn't even turn to answer. The little bun wobbled back and forth as she shook her head. If Barruci's didn't have the finest wine list in this corner of London, he'd have boycotted the place weeks ago. But it was the best little restaurant in the suburb of Vinehurst, right on the fringes of London's urban sprawl. A few minutes' drive to the south and it was all countryside. Vinehurst had probably once been an idyllic little village, with its narrow cobbled high street, a Norman church and an old-fashioned cricket pitch that was still used every Sunday. Somehow, during the last century, as London had spread, it hadn't swallowed up Vinehurst, as it had similar hamlets and towns. There was a distinct absence of grey concrete and high-rise buildings, as if the city had just flowed round the village, leaving a little bubble of rural charm behind. It was a great place for a first date.

At eight o'clock on the dot, a woman walked into the restaurant.

It was her.

The dark wavy hair was coiled behind her head somehow and she wore a neat black coat, fitted at the waist. Even though he was too far away to tell if her eyes were really the same colour as her profile photograph, they drew his attention—bright and alert, scanning the room beneath quirkily arched brows. He watched as her gaze flitted from one table to the next, pausing for a split-second on the men, then moving on when she saw they weren't alone.

Noah put down the menu he'd been perusing and sat up straighter, giving no indication that his heart was beating just a little bit faster. Could the hamsters at Blinddatebrides.com finally have got it right?

Finally, the woman leaned over and whispered something to a waitress. The girl nodded and waited as the woman stopped to remove her coat. There was a collective pause as every man in the place held his breath for a heartbeat, then pretended to resume conversation with their friends, wives or girlfriends. In reality, they were tracking the woman's progress across the room. Even the ones who were far too young for her.

Under the respectable coat was a stunning dress. The same shade and sheen as a peacock's body. The scoop neck wasn't even close to being indecent, but somehow it didn't need to be. It teased very nicely while it sat there, revealing not even a hint of cleavage. The hem was short and the legs, the legs…

Well, the legs hadn't been visible in the Blind-datebrides.com photo, but they were very nice indeed. Too nice, maybe. Maybe she was a vixen incognito. He loosened his tie slightly and tried to smile as she followed the waitress through the maze of tables, leaving a trail of wistful male eyes in her wake. The smile felt forced and he abandoned it. He didn't do small talk; he did conversation. And he didn't do overly effusive greetings these days, even in the presence of such fine legs.

When the waitress pulled out the chair opposite

him for her, he stood and offered his hand. 'Noah…Smith.' A necessary diversion from the truth if he was to gauge if his dates really liked him for his personality rather than his bank balance. Sometimes he wished he'd had enough sense to use a pen name, but the lure of seeing 'Noah Frost' stamped in square letters across the front of a book jacket had been too great after all the years of rejections.

'Hello,' she said, shaking his hand, then quickly pulling hers away again. 'You've got really nice teeth.'

He opened his mouth to say, *All the better to eat you with,* but managed to stop himself. Instead, he just kept quiet and motioned for her to sit down. He did the same.

'Nice teeth?' he said, smiling again. 'Do you want to check my hooves to see if I'm good stock too?'

She blushed ever so slightly and the mischievous little smile from the profile photograph made an appearance.

'Grace Marlowe—blind-date virgin…' She clapped a hand over her mouth. It looked as if she were trying to wipe a cheeky smile away as she dragged her hand over her lips and let it fall. It didn't work. The grin popped back into place as if nothing had happened.

'That came out all wrong. What I meant was…this will be my first time.'

She closed her eyes and bit her lip. Without opening

her lids, she kept speaking. 'I'm making it worse, aren't I—digging myself an even deeper hole?'

Noah stared at her. This wasn't how the other dates had started. Where was the murmured conversation, the polite questioning as to jobs and musical tastes?

'It's only because I'm more of a blind-date veteran that I'm not in there with a matching shovel.'

She opened one eye. 'You're nice, Mr Smith. And chivalrous to a lady in distress.' The other eye popped open and she tipped her head to one side. 'How come you've had so many first dates if you're such a nice guy? What's wrong with you?'

Now it was his turn to laugh. His male pride really ought to be dented. None of his other dates had been so blunt. But none of his other dates had been quite so interesting.

'This is only the fourth date I've been on.'

'In how long?'

He shrugged. 'A month?'

'That's a lot of ladies who passed you by, Noah. Tell me why I shouldn't follow the crowd.'

Despite the fact that he was known for his cool, unruffled demeanour, he found himself laughing again.

'I've got nice teeth?'

'There is that,' she said, her eyes twinkling. And they really were that blue. She looked at the tablecloth and scratched at a catch in the linen. 'Sorry about the teeth thing. I was a little nervous, and when I'm nervous I tend to say the first thing that pops into my head.'

Although it seemed to get her into trouble, he found it quite endearing. And refreshing. The more successful he'd become, the more people second-guessed their every word around him. Getting an honest reaction—rather than one that had been carefully edited before it left a person's mouth—was a wonderful novelty.

'Shall we order?'

She breathed out a sigh, making a little round shape with her mouth. 'That would be lovely.'

He opened the large, unwieldy menu and scanned it, even though he was pretty sure he was going to start with the carpaccio of beef and follow it with the scallops.

'We can discuss my many faults over the appetisers,' he said, completely deadpan.

The bright eyes appeared above the menu, laughing at him. Noah smiled to himself and paid careful attention. You could tell a lot about a person from what food they ordered. She chose the beef too. Another good sign.

No. Not a sign—he didn't believe in signs. Just an indicator of compatibility.

She let him choose the wine and, by the time he'd narrowed the choices down to match their courses, their appetisers had arrived.

'So, what do you do, Grace?'

She looked up from her salad—not by raising her head, but by looking at him through her lashes. A flicker of emotion passed across her face and she popped a piece of avocado in her mouth. Didn't she want to tell him what she did for a living? It couldn't be as bad as last Saturday's date. A pet psychologist, for goodness' sake!

When Grace finished chewing, she mumbled, 'I'm a barrister.'

Not quite what he'd expected. He wondered if she'd be too tied down to her job to think about travelling with him. That might be a deal-breaker.

'How about you? What do you do for a living?'

He opened his mouth and closed it again. Time to learn from past mistakes. The moment he mentioned thrillers and novel-writing, the game was normally up. Noah wasn't a particularly common name and people tended to guess the connection, even if he used his totally imaginative Noah Smith alias. And he didn't want Grace to go all giggly and stupid like some women did.

'You do have a job at the moment, don't you?' Grace said.

'Of course I do. I'm a writer.'

To his relief, Grace looked pleasantly unimpressed. 'What kind of writer?'

He shrugged. 'I write about military stuff. Quite boring, actually.' Another little detour.

Grace dabbed her mouth with her napkin. 'Are you pulling my leg?'

Rats. She could tell he was fudging the issue. Just as well he hadn't decided to be an actor instead of a novelist. At least his characters were convincing, even if he wasn't.

'No,' he said with his best poker face.

Grace looked at him long and hard. Had she guessed his secret? If she had, she wasn't smiling and going all gooey, which was unusual.

'So, tell me about your other dates,' she said, her eyes never leaving his face. 'What went wrong?'

'Nothing.' He took a deep breath and let his face relax out of his smile. 'But it's a serious business, finding a wife. I'm not going to trot off down the aisle with just anyone.'

She put her knife and fork down and stared at her salad for a few seconds. 'You're really looking for a wife on an Internet dating site?'

Why did his dates seem to find that so hard to believe? After all, the site in question was Blind-datebrides.com. It kind of gave the game away.

'Aren't you looking for a husband?'

Grace shook her head hard to loosen her hairdo a little.

'What are you looking for, then? Love? A soulmate?'

She dropped her chin and gave him an *Are you serious?* look from under her lashes.

Good. She didn't believe in those things either.

'I'm glad we're on the same wavelength,' he said before taking a sip of wine.

Grace pursed her lips. 'It's not that I don't believe in those things. Just that I'm not expecting to find them at Blinddatebrides.com. Nor do I want to. I mean, the whole Romeo and Juliet, all-consuming passion thing really only works for teenagers, don't you think?'

He raised his eyebrows in what he hoped was a non-committal way. He wasn't sure what this 'in love' thing was. Oh, he'd thought he'd found it once, but it had turned out to be a case of mistaken identity. What people sang about in love songs or wept over at the cinema wasn't real. It was all an illusion—one he bought into about as much as he had the chick with the AK47.

His parents didn't do all that hearts and flowers nonsense and they had been perfectly happy for almost fifty years. If it could work for them, it could work for him.

The evening passed quickly. Too quickly.

As Noah dug into his dessert, he decided he'd seen enough of Grace to know she wasn't what Harry termed a 'WAG wannabe' in disguise—definitely not a gold-digger! There was a recital at one of the local arts centres next week that he'd planned on going to, and he was going to ask Grace if she'd like to go with him.

He cleared his throat. 'Grace?'

She looked up at him, a chocolate-dipped spoon half in her mouth. Slowly, and while Noah's mouth began to water, she pulled it out, sucking the last of the rich brown mousse off.

'Do you want some?' she asked, eyebrows raised, mouth slightly smudged with chocolate. Noah meant to shake his head, but it didn't seem to want to move.

'Uh-huh,' he heard himself say.

'It is rather divine,' she said, her eyes doing her trademark sparkle.

'Uh-huh.'

Great. He'd won awards for his command of the English language and all he could do at present was grunt like a caveman. He watched as she carefully dipped the long spoon into her dessert and pulled out a bulging dollop of creamy chocolate mousse.

As she fed him the mousse, she unconsciously licked her lips. Noah felt a kick of desire so hard it almost rocked him out of his chair. His voice was horribly hoarse when he opened his mouth to speak. 'Grace…?'

'Yes.'

'Um…' Just like that, his brain emptied. Words circled round, but the ability to string them into coherent sentences had just vanished. He grabbed at a few of the nearest phrases in desperation. 'Concerts!' he blurted. 'Do you like live music?'

Grace's face lit up. 'I *love* live music!'

It was only as his heart rate started to slow, pounding heavily in his temples, that he realised it had been racing for the last couple of minutes. He swallowed, which really wasn't a good idea, because he tasted the chocolate mousse again and his pulse did a U-turn.

'In fact, I was only at a concert a few days ago,' Grace said, before turning her attention back to her dessert.

'Really?'

She nodded and swallowed. 'I saw this great band up in London recently—The Hover Cats—have you heard of them?'

He shook his head.

'I don't expect many of your colleagues share your passion, do they?'

She looked puzzled. 'Why not? I know jazz and easy listening are popular in cafés, but that's not all we listen to. Aren't you being just a little bit narrow-minded?'

For the second time that evening, Noah felt as if he were under interrogation. 'But I thought you said you were a—'

'A barista,' she said, folding her arms. 'I work in The Coffee Bean further up the High Street.'

If she'd jumped up on the table and started doing the can-can, Noah couldn't have been more shocked. She had such potential. And all at once he was intrigued, as he often was when he met some-one who defied his expectations. What had led her to make those choices? Grace had the personality and energy to do anything she wanted. His brain whirred off, analysing her as if she were a charac-ter in a book.

She'd been sitting in silence as he'd absorbed the information, but now she flicked a glance at the door and started talking very fast. 'Talking of coffee, I don't really feel like having one—busman's holiday and all that. Do you mind if we call it a night?'

She reached for her handbag and started to push back her seat. For the first time all evening, the confidence, the pizzazz drained away. She glanced at him for a mere moment as she smoothed down her skirt and he saw a look of both hardness and vulnerability on her face.

'Grace, I'm sorry. In no way do I—' He reached for her hand. 'Don't go.'

She shook her head. 'You know what, Noah. This really isn't going to work out. I think I should just leave.' And, with that, she nimbly eased herself out of her chair and headed for the coat rack.

Known for his command of the English language? Hah.

Well, if Grace was leaving, so was he. He pulled his wallet out of his pocket, left more than enough twenty pound notes on the table to cover the bill and darted after her.

* * *

Grace didn't even remember putting her coat on. It was only as the chilly night air hit her face that her brain whirred into action. Without making a conscious decision, she turned right and hurried down Vinehurst High Street as fast as the stupid high heels she'd stolen out the bottom of Daisy's wardrobe would let her.

'Grace!'

She bit the tip of her tongue between her teeth, shook her head and just kept walking. Every time she told people what she did for a living she got the same reaction, the same look. The one that said, why wasn't she busy saving lives on the operating table or running a million-pound Internet business she'd started in her front room like other women of her generation?

Because she hadn't been prepared to sacrifice time with Daisy to build a career, that was why. Daisy had already lost one parent and she didn't need the other to become a dim and distant memory while childminders did all the hands-on stuff. So Grace had taken a job that let her fit her hours round the school day and didn't require evening shifts.

The owner of the coffee shop was Aunt Caroline—or Caz, as she liked to be called. She was really Rob's aunt, but had welcomed Grace into the family with open arms and had been a lifesaver when he'd died, taking Grace under her wing and letting her rent the upstairs flat. Grace's parents had moved to the West Country when she'd got married and there had been no one close by to turn to. Her parents had begged her to move in with them, but she'd refused—too young, foolish and independent at the time to realise what a gift it might have been. But Rob was buried in the churchyard here and she hadn't been able to wrench herself away, leave him behind.

She became aware of someone following her and picked up speed. She shouldn't be made to feel ashamed of her job. She made the best pastries in the area. And, even if she hadn't, she didn't want to apologise for her work.

She could hear heavy, pounding footsteps behind her now. Just for a while, she'd thought she'd been having a decent conversation with someone who didn't assume she had an IQ of twenty because she baked and served coffee for a living. And he'd been nice to her…But only because he'd misheard her and thought she was something she wasn't.

'Grace!'

He was right behind her now. She stopped and turned round, hardening herself, putting on that sassy front she used with difficult customers at The Coffee Bean. 'Mr Smith.'

'Grace, you got me all wrong! I don't care if you work in a coffee shop or a lawyer's office. I don't want the night to end this way, do you?'

No, she didn't. Adult company, a little bit of sophistication, had been nice. And she'd thought Noah had been gorgeous too, right up until the end. But he'd come after her. That was quite nice. To be exact, he'd run after her. And they had been having fun.

She started walking again. 'What if I worked as a litter picker? Would you still have come after me?'

His features shifted and changed. When they'd been sitting down in the restaurant, she hadn't noticed how tall he was. Now, she had to tilt her head up to get a look in his eyes.

They were the most beautiful colour. Green. Not the emerald-green of story books, but a cool, glassy green that verged on grey. Even so, their paleness didn't detract from their intensity. When he looked at her she felt as if she had one hundred per cent of his attention, as if she were the only thing in his field of focus. But now they didn't seem focused, they seemed puzzled.

'Of course, I'd have come after you. I came out for a nice dinner and ended up chewing my own size twelve shoes. I needed to apologise.'

He wasn't taking the bait, playing her little game, but his honesty won her over. She didn't have time for slimy men who oozed the right things. She'd settle for Noah Smith and his no-nonsense words—even if they were occasionally muffled by his shoe leather. Had he really said size *twelves*…?

He fell into step beside her. 'So, are we okay? Do you want to go somewhere for coff—a drink?'

She smiled. 'How about if I was a sewage worker? Would you want to have a drink with me then?'

There was a tiny break in the rhythm of his steps. 'Only if I was allowed to wear a peg on my nose.'

Her tense jaw muscles relaxed and a smile she'd been anchoring down sprung up. Finally, he'd joined her game. She grabbed his hand and speeded up. 'Come on. I know the perfect place.'

Noah had no choice but to follow Grace as her shoes measured out rapid little steps. Even in heels, she only just reached past his shoulders and he didn't have to do more than stroll to keep up.

The sky glowed a murky pink, reflecting the street lamps of a vast city. Typical for a spring night in England, an icy splosh of rain hit the top of his head, not even deflected by his hair. If he and Grace didn't hurry up, they were about to get soaked. Just as he opened his mouth to ask where they were going, she dragged him into a doorway.

Out of the wind whistling down the High Street, the air was surprisingly close. Grace was only inches away, smiling up at him cheekily. He took a deep breath. It didn't matter that the rain was now falling out of the sky and his right arm, out of the cover of the small doorway, was getting wet. All that mattered was the slight shine cast on her lips by the street lamp on the other side of the road. He couldn't stop looking at them. The smile faded from her face and she regarded him with wide eyes.

The sound of the rain slapping against the pavement seemed to grow and intensify until it filled his ears. He knew he was about to lean forward and kiss her. Not that he'd made a decision; somehow he just knew. And there was nothing he could do to stop himself.

Just as his muscles prepared themselves for movement, he heard a jangle of keys and suddenly Grace was gone. He looked in confusion at the open door and listened to her heels track their way across the darkened shop. Attempting to follow was a bad idea, he discovered, sending a chair flying and leaving himself with a throbbing shin.

'Hang on a moment,' Grace said from somewhere in the darkness.

A few seconds later a light went on above a counter on the other side of the room. As his eyes adjusted to the blackness, a thunderclap rumbled a few miles away. Grace skirted round the tables and closed the door. She didn't say anything as she moved past him; it was only as she was walking away back to the counter that she spoke.

'This place serves the best coffee in the whole of South East London.'

Now he noticed his surroundings. The place

almost resembled an auction room with its assorted wooden tables and chairs—no two matching. Large velvet-covered sofas occupied one corner and big canvases of abstract art and pictures of coffee beans hung on the walls.

'The best?'

Now Grace was more than ten feet away and standing behind the safety of a counter she seemed to have regained her usual chatty manner. 'Absolutely. And I know that because I make it. What will you have?'

'Espresso,' he said without thinking. 'Double.'

'Coming right up. Make yourself at home.' He moved towards one of the low armchairs near the counter and sat down as Grace began banging things and turning knobs. A minute or so later she joined him with two cups of steaming espresso. The smell of freshly ground coffee filled the air like a fog. They sat and sipped their drinks in silence.

Grace hadn't switched any extra lights on and they were sitting on the fringes of the yellow glow from the counter. Even in this artificial twilight she seemed brighter and bolder and more alive than just about anyone he knew.

'So, Noah…How does a guy like you end up listed on an Internet dating site? If you don't mind me saying, I wouldn't have thought it was…you know…your thing, or that you needed help in that department.'

Noah considered what she'd said for a moment, then smiled.

'I decided that meeting people via the Internet was as good a way as any. It's all down to chance, really. You meet someone in a bar, or at work, or wherever…Why not the Internet? Joining a site with a matching service should help take some of the guesswork out of it.'

Grace rolled her eyes. 'You make it all sound so romantic!'

Romance. What was that, anyway? He, like most men, had thought it meant flowers and chocolates and candlelit dinners. That much he could manage. In the five years he'd been with Sara, the one woman he'd thought of marrying without the help of a dating site, she'd tried to explain that romance was more about connecting with someone on a deeper level, about seeing into someone's soul. He'd nodded and looked thoughtful and, although he'd tried hard to understand, he'd had the funny feeling he'd missed the point. Even though he'd *connected* to the best of his abilities she'd still walked away, telling him it wasn't enough. The truly tragic thing was that he honestly didn't know what he could have done differently.

Noah stared out of the plate glass window at the front of the shop. It was raining hard now, fat drops bouncing off the road and swirling down the gutters. That kind of romance was the last place to start if you wanted a successful relationship.

When he looked back at Grace that cheeky eyebrow rose again. How could she say so much with one small twitch of a muscle?

'Don't you believe in fate, in destiny?' she asked.

Noah didn't even have to stop and think about that one. 'No.'

'So it's all just down to random events and chemical reactions, then?'

'Well, partly…at least, I think that's what sexual attraction boils down to, but we're not just talking about that. Choosing someone to spend your life with is about more than chemistry, surely? Why? Do you believe in fate?'

Grace put her cup down and looked at the ceiling. 'I don't know…It's comforting to think that love isn't just some random genetic thing. Where's the magic in that?'

Uh-oh. If she was looking for magic, she was barking up the wrong tree. He didn't do magic any more than he did romance. Loyalty, honesty, sheer bloody-mindedness—he had those things in spades, but there wasn't any fairy dust involved. It was just the way he was made. Time to get things back on firmer ground. Time to return to facts and figures and things a man could quantify.

'Why did you join Blinddatebrides.com?'

Grace looked at the ceiling and shook her head. 'Actually, I'd never heard of the site before this morning. Someone else joined on my behalf and

I'm going to kill her when I get my hands…' She bit her lip and grimaced. 'Sorry. That didn't sound the way I meant it to. I didn't want to imply that I regret meeting you.'

'Of course you didn't.'

He liked the way she didn't filter her words.

'Maybe I'll let her off with dunking her in the old horse trough on the common…Now that I've discovered having a blind date isn't quite as horrendous as I anticipated.'

The corner of his mouth twitched. 'I'm flattered. Me having such fine teeth, and all. You will tell your friend about the teeth, won't you?'

Grace put down her coffee cup. 'Oh, it wasn't a friend who set me up. It was my daughter.'

His stomach plummeted just that little bit further. He hadn't even considered that Grace might have children. She just looked too…And he was useless with kids. His friends' kids only tolerated him when he visited because, on occasion, he could be coaxed into letting them ride on his shoulders. Any attempts at communication just fell flat. They would stare at him with their mouths open as if he were an alien life form. No, Noah and kids just didn't mix.

'You have a daughter?' he asked, consciously trying to keep his tone light.

She nodded. 'Daisy. Nineteen—the age when she thinks Mama doesn't know best any more and is doing her best to organise my life to her liking.'

See? Nineteen was better. He might be able to manage children—well, young adults—at that age.

'So, you're divorced?'

She shook her head. 'Widowed.' Her hand flew up. 'Don't give me the look!'

He blinked. What look?

'It was a long time ago. I was barely more than a teenager when I got married and not much older when I found myself on my own again.' She gave him a fierce look, one that dared him to feel sorry for her.

'How did he die?'

Grace went very quiet. Was he tasting his own shoe polish again?

'Thank you for asking. Most people just…you know…change the subject.' She tipped her chin up and looked straight at him. 'Rob was a soldier. He was killed in the first Gulf War.'

Noah nodded. 'I served in Iraq myself.'

She pressed her lips together and gave him a watery smile. He didn't have the words to describe what happened next; he just felt a bolt of recognition joining them together in silent understanding. So many friends hadn't made it home. And he'd seen so many wives fall apart. But here was Grace, not letting the world defeat her. She'd worked hard to bring her daughter up on her own. It couldn't have been easy. And he'd bet she was a really good mother, one who had strived to be both mother and father to her daughter. If only every child were so lucky. He almost felt jealous of the absent Daisy.

This was getting far too emotional for him, pulling on loose threads of things he'd firmly locked away in his subconscious. Grace wasn't looking for the same kind of relationship he was. She didn't want to get married and, if she did, she wanted magic. His instincts told him it was time to retreat and let them both breathe out.

'Well, Grace…' He swallowed the last of his espresso and stood up. 'I think I'd better be going.' He shrugged. 'Can I call you a cab or give you a lift somewhere?'

She shook her head. 'No need. I am home. I live in the flat upstairs.'

Well, he hadn't been expecting that. It kind of left him with nowhere to go.

'It's been nice…'

A small smile curved her lips. 'Yes it has.'

The words *See you again some time?* were ready on the tip of his tongue. He swallowed them. But once they were gone he had nothing else to say, so he walked to the door, aware of her following close behind him. When they reached it, she flicked a couple of catches and turned the handle, oddly silent.

Before he crossed the threshold into the damp night he turned to look at her. 'It was lovely to meet you, Grace.'

'So you already said.'

He took a step backwards beyond the shelter of the doorway and the rain hit him in multiple wet stabs. He shuddered. For an instant, rational thought hadn't come into it—he was only aware of his body's physical response to the drop in temperature, the cold water running down his skin.

Grace stood in the doorway, in front of one of the angled panes of glass, her eyes large and round. All the laughter had left them now, but they were focused intently on him.

'Bye, Noah,' she said, and looked down at the floor.

Suddenly, he was moving. He took two long steps until he was standing in front of her and, without stopping to explain or analyse, he placed a hand either side of her head on the window and leaned in close. Her lips parted and she sank back against the pane and jerkily took in some air.

And then he kissed Grace the way he'd wanted to all evening.

CHAPTER THREE

GRACE clung to Noah for support. She had to. If she released the lapels of his jacket, she'd be in serious danger of sliding down the glass and landing in a heap at his feet.

It had been quite a long time since she'd been kissed. Perhaps the memories were a little fuzzy, but she didn't think she remembered it being this good. Every part of her seemed to be going gooey. And he wasn't even using his hands. They were still pressed against the glass as he towered over her and it was merely the brushing, teasing, coaxing of his lips that was making her feel this way.

She'd never been kissed like this before. Never.

And with that thought an icy chill ran through her.

Surely Rob's kisses had excited her like this? He *had* to come top of her list. He was Daisy's father, her soulmate, her grand passion. Anyone else would only ever be second place. But when she thought of him, she could remember youthful exuberance, raw need, but never this devastating skill that was threatening to…

Her fingers unclenched and she laid her palms flat against Noah's chest, intending to apply gentle pressure as a signal that she wanted him to stop. But she didn't stop him. Noah chose that moment to run his tongue along her lip and she moaned gently, reached behind his neck with both hands and pulled him closer.

When Noah's hands finally moved off the window and started stroking the tingling skin of her neck, her cheeks, that little hollow at the base of her throat, she stopped thinking altogether. And she had no idea how long they'd been necking in the doorway like teenagers when he finally pulled away.

She was shaking—literally quivering—as he stood there looking down at her with his pale eyes. His thumb was still tracing the line of her cheekbone. Just that alone made the skin behind her ears sizzle.

This was so *not* what she'd been expecting on her first date. The chat rooms on Blinddatebrides.com that afternoon had been full of stories of nerdy guys and boring evenings, lots of jokes about kissing frogs. After getting her head around Daisy's whole madcap plan, that was what she'd been anticipating. She'd been expecting to feel a sense of relief that the ordeal was over, to chalk it up to experience and carry on with her life. She certainly hadn't been expecting to feel *this*.

'Grace?'

Even his whisper was sexy. Low and growly. She tried not to shiver more than she already was doing.

'I'd really like to see you again.'

Her body was telling her to yell *yes*, drag him back into the coffee shop and make use of one of those squashy sofas. And just that thought alone was enough to throw a bucket of cold water all over her. She didn't *do* one-night stands, or necking in doorways. She did *soulmates* and *love at first sight*—with marriage and baby rapidly following. This wasn't for her. Blinddatebrides.com wasn't for her.

She wriggled out of Noah's arms and retreated behind the door, using it as a shield as she held it half-closed. 'I'm sorry, Noah. I just don't think that's a good idea.' And before she could talk herself out of it, she shut the door, flipped the catches and walked through the shop without looking back.

Noah stared at Grace as she disappeared into the barely lit café. In the gloom, she became a dark grey blob, then, suddenly, the interior of The Coffee Bean was plunged into darkness.

He just kept on staring, even though he was now staring at his own reflection in the glass. The one woman he'd found who'd really caught his interest had just given him the brush-off. He couldn't remember the last time that had happened in the previous five years. The irony of it hit him so hard he started to chuckle.

Aware that the pubs were emptying and people were starting to fill the High Street, he pulled himself together. Men who stood and laughed at their reflections in shop windows were likely to be carted down to the local police station to sleep it off.

He looked himself in the eyes.

Well done, Mr Best-selling Author. You've finally found the secret to repelling women: be interested.

The narrow flight of stairs that led up to her flat seemed especially steep this evening. Grace opened the door at the top and, once she'd taken her coat off, she looked down at herself. Who was she kidding? In Daisy's prom dress and Daisy's shoes, she looked like someone playing dressing-up.

Sophisticated? I don't think so!

She stripped the clothes and the stockings off right where she stood and marched into the bedroom to find her pyjamas. Once dressed in her striped three-quarter length trousers and vest top, she stood, hands on her hips, and glared round her room. It was cluttered with lotions and potions, clothes borrowed from Daisy and clothes Daisy had returned.

There was no point trying to go to sleep. Not going to happen.

She fetched Daisy's laptop and took it into the sitting room, where she collapsed onto the sofa with it. Once it had booted up, she logged into Blinddatebrides.com.

Blinddatebrides.com is running 12 chat rooms, 36 private Instant Messaging conferences, and 4233 members are online. Chat with your dating prospects now!

Grace clicked on the 'New to the site' chatroom where she'd found Kangagirl and Sanfrandani earlier on, but none of the names listed in the conversation were theirs. She shook her head. It had to be midday in Australia and she had absolutely no idea what time it would be on the west coast of America. Sanfrandani was probably fast asleep.

She was about to turn the blasted machine off when it beeped at her and a little window popped up.

Kangagirl is inviting you to a private IM conference. Click OK to accept the invitation.

Grace didn't hesitate. Another window popped up.

Kangagirl: You're back! Tell us how it went!
Englishcrumpet: Us?
Sanfrandani: I'm here too!
Englishcrumpet: Shouldn't you be in bed?

Sanfrandani: LOL! Only if I want to get fired. It's three o'clock in the afternoon!
Englishcrumpet: Oh.
Kangagirl: So...
Sanfrandani: Yes! Juicy details please!

Juicy details indeed. There *were* no juicy details. It had just been a kiss.

Yeah, right. And caramel moccachino was just plain coffee.

Englishcrumpet: We had dinner and coffee and then he left.
Sanfrandani: The question is: are you going to see him again?
Englishcrumpet: I don't think so.
Kangagirl: Didn't he ask?

Grace's fingers hovered above the keys. It was so tempting just to type *no* and save herself all the post-mortems. But these girls had been really helpful when she'd needed them this morning and she just couldn't lie to them.

Englishcrumpet: He asked. I said no.
Kangagirl: What was he like?
Sanfrandani: Big fat loser?

Grace shook her head. That would have been so much easier. She'd been out to a beautiful restaurant with a charming, cultured man, who kissed like a dream, and she'd done a runner? How did she explain that without seeming stark raving bonkers?

Englishcrumpet: I don't think we were a good match. He was too...
Kangagirl: Boring?
Sanfrandani: Old?
Kangagirl: Weird?
Sanfrandani: Big-headed?
Kangagirl: Come on, Englishcrumpet! Help us out here!

She blew out a breath. None of those descriptions applied to Noah. How did she put it into words?

Englishcrumpet: He was too much of a 'grown-up'.

Too much of a lot of things, but that was all she could put her finger on right now.
Kangagirl: And you—if you don't mind me asking—are the grand old age of...?
Sanfrandani: Kangagirl! You can't ask that!
Kangagirl: I'm Australian. It's practically my birthright to be blunt.
Englishcrumpet: I'm...thirty-ten.
Kangagirl: Huh?
Englishcrumpet: Think of 30 and add 10. I refuse to use the 'f' word.

Sanfrandani: Crumpet, you're a hoot!
Kangagirl: What was he, then? A senior citizen?
Englishcrumpet: It was more about lifestyle than about age. I hang out with my daughter and her teenage friends. So I like takeaways and bad horror movies and reading Cosmo. *He was a foodie, into opera and military history books.*
Kangagirl: Not your cup of tea, Crumpet?
Englishcrumpet: Very funny!
Sanfrandani: So…your search for true love hit a road bump?

Grace typed the next reply so fast she surprised herself.

Englishcrumpet: I'm not looking for true love.
For a few seconds, nothing happened. The cursor just blinked at her.

Sanfrandani: Don't believe in it?
Kangagirl: You're on the wrong website, then!
Englishcrumpet: I do *believe in true love, it's just…*

How did she explain? She knew true love existed, because she'd had it with Rob.

Englishcrumpet: I just don't think you can have that kind of connection twice in a lifetime.

Sanfrandani: I see.
Kangagirl: Oh. Hugs, Englishcrumpet.

Rob had been her other half. How could anyone else take his place? And she didn't know if she could settle for less. Even if she was lonely sometimes. Even if, secretly, in a dark place where she didn't even want to admit it to herself, she was a little bit jealous of the easy companionship Daisy had had with her last serious boyfriend.

Sanfrandani: How about dating with the idea of finding someone to share your life with? Even if it's not the meant-to-be-in-the-stars kind of love?

Grace sat back in the sofa and stared at the screen. Sanfrandani had a point. Just because it wasn't going to be the same as she'd had with Rob, it didn't mean she couldn't find a different kind of happiness with someone else. That was what Noah had been talking about, hadn't he? Could she see herself making that kind of mature, adult decision about a relationship?

Englishcrumpet: I don't know. Maybe.

The Coffee Bean was virtually empty, as it normally was on a Sunday morning before the shoppers were out in full force. It was Grace's ritual to treat herself to breakfast down here just one day a week—any more than that and she'd be the size of a house. Around ten-thirty, she crawled down the stairs from her flat, propped herself against the counter and yawned so hard she thought her jaw might dislocate.

Caz was resplendent this morning in a lurid Paisley kaftan, her silver-blonde hair caught into a loose bun that looked as if it might disintegrate under its own weight at any second. The owner truly was as original as her kooky little café.

Caz looked her up and down. 'Either you've had a really terrible night or a *really* good one. Which was it?'

That was the point. Grace wasn't quite sure. Whichever it had been, insomnia had come as part of the package.

'A tall skinny latte with two shots, please.'

Caz winked at her. 'Say no more. Coming right up.'

Grace yawned again and looked round the café. It was a charming place, full of interesting knick-knacks. Old enamel jugs sat on random tables, filled with daffodils. Old road signs and mirrors covered the walls. Best of all was the ornate Victorian mahogany counter, still with some of the original etched glass, that filled one side of the café and the black and white tiled floor—a reminder of its former life as a butchers. The Coffee Bean always smelled of something comforting. The locals loved it but, with two new coffee houses on the High Street—both international chains—they were feeling the pinch.

But the buying public obviously were dull enough to enjoy the same old plastic-wrapped nonsense in whatever town they were in. The same menu of coffees. The Coffee Bean was unique, with an ever-changing menu and warm staff who really loved their jobs. But, unfortunately, that didn't stop the profit margins falling and the costs going up.

Caroline handed Grace her coffee and returned to frowning over some printed-off spreadsheets.

'How are this week's figures?'

Caz shuffled the papers and tucked them under the till.

'Come on, Caz. I'm family. And I'm supposed to be your assistant manageress. Even if you keep the happy, smiley face for the other staff, put me in the picture.'

The other woman shook her head. 'It doesn't matter what we do. Java Express is running promotion after promotion.' She shrugged. 'If things don't pick up, we'll be out of business in three months.'

Grace put her coffee down, marched around the counter and flung her arms round Caz, ignoring the overpowering scent of lavender and the flakes of dandruff liberally salting her shoulders. There was no way she was going to let The Coffee Bean close. It was like a member of the Marlowe family.

She'd first met Rob here, when he'd had a Saturday job with his aunt. A couple of years later, when her dad had consented to let her start dating, it had been the venue for her first date. Caz had even made their wedding cake.

Daisy had slept in her pram near the back door on many occasions as a baby. The customers had spent many an hour when she was a toddler admiring her drawings and sneaking her bits of cake. Later, when she'd been older, she'd done her homework on the little table in the corner every night. The regulars all loved her and had insisted on trying to help her, even if they'd always come up with different answers for her questions and spent more time arguing with each other than actually being any use with equations or the dates of famous battles.

Too many happy memories. And now Daisy and Rob were gone and The Coffee Bean and her memories were all she had left. She wasn't going to let them be hoovered up by a big corporation without a fight.

'We'll find a way. I'll create a new cake—one so spectacular it'll stop people in the street and force them to dive in and buy some.'

Caz patted her on the arm and pulled away. 'Amazing as your creations are, my flower, I don't think they're a match for Java Express's "buy one get one free"s on just about everything.' She shook her head. 'Trouble is, nobody wants to pay for quality any more. They want everything for half the price it was last year.'

'I've got my savings. Only a few thousand, but still…'

Caz folded her arms and shook her head. 'No way. You've been saving for long enough to open your own shop. I can't take that away from you.'

'But I could be a partner in *this* shop, couldn't I? You offered that to me once.'

Caz's eyes became glassy. 'Bless you, Grace, but no. We both know the chance of saving The Coffee Bean is slim, and you might need that money for university fees for Daisy. I can't let you plug a hole in a sinking ship and lose your nest egg in the process.'

'I want to, Caz. You know how much this place means to me.'

'Sorry, Grace. Can't let you do it.'

Grace gave Caz a rueful smile and rubbed her arm. 'I'll try to find a way to make you, you know.'

Caz chuckled. 'I know you will. But I've had a good twenty years longer at perfecting my stubbornness.'

Grace opened her mouth to argue, but at that moment the old-fashioned bell on the café door jingled and both women turned to look at who had just walked in.

'Oh, my goodness!' Grace put her hands over her mouth.

She couldn't even see the delivery boy behind the largest bunch of flowers in the history of the universe.

His voice came out muffled from behind all the greenery. 'Grace Marlowe?'

Grace let out a squeak.

'Over there,' Caz said, gesticulating first towards Grace and then to one of the free tables. The boy carefully lowered the bouquet and stumbled free of the foliage.

Grace couldn't take her eyes off the huge bunch of flowers as she squiggled her name on the boy's clipboard. Nothing as unimaginative and predictable as lilies or roses. These were large architectural flowers—some of which she couldn't even put a name to—framed with angular leaves and rapier-sharp grasses. And the smell…

'Someone really did have a good night last night, didn't they?' Caz was standing back behind the counter, her arms folded across her ample chest. 'Go on, then. Look at the card.'

Grace didn't need to look at the card. No one had sent her flowers in a long time. Even Rob had only managed a bunch of petrol station roses on the night he'd proposed. One of the heads had fallen off, but he'd been nineteen and she'd been eighteen and, at the time, they'd been the most beautiful things she'd ever seen. Of course, they paled in comparison to Noah's bouquet. Somehow, she wished he had sent her lilies. It would have been easier to dismiss them, easier to put Rob's eleven roses and one sad stalk in first place.

She scowled as she searched for the card amongst the tissue paper and sharp grasses.

> *To Grace,*
> *Thank you for an unforgettable evening.*
> *Noah.*

Grace blew out a breath. She didn't like this warm feeling spreading through her bones. How was she supposed to forget that kiss with these flowers stinking out her flat for the next week? Two weeks, probably. They came from one of the most expensive florists in town and looked like the sort of blooms that didn't need gallons of water.

She picked up the bouquet and rustled over to Caz. 'Here, you have them,' she said and dumped them on the counter.

Caz just folded her arms tighter and shook her head. Grace shoved them an inch or two closer.

'Go on. They're far too posh for me. They'll look out of place in my little flat. Have them for the café.'

Caz just raised her eyebrows.

'You're impossible,' Grace said and flounced off

to find some scissors and spare jugs. When she
returned she hauled the bouquet onto one of the
larger tables and set about slicing through the cellophane and trimming the stems.

'Evict the daffodils from my jugs and I'll dock
your pay.'

Grace turned and stared at Caz open-mouthed.
'You wouldn't.'

Caz just blinked.

'I'll take you to Industrial Tribunal,' Grace added,
picking up a large green thing and trying to work
out if it was a flower or just an ornate leaf.

'Fine,' came the reply. 'Do it. But by the time it
gets sorted, I'll probably be out of business and
you will get an award of big fat zero.'

Grace's eyes became slits. 'Like I said—impossible!'

'It's high time you let a man buy you flowers. So,
sorry, you're stuck with them.'

Well, she'd see about that.

The computer whirred and, after a few seconds,
pinged cheerfully at Noah. He looked up from his
Sunday crossword and scanned the list of emails
that had just arrived in his inbox.

A stab of guilt hit him as he spotted one from his
mother, inviting him to Sunday lunch the following
week. It had been a while since he'd made the trip
to the coast. In his opinion, relationships with

parents were best conducted from afar—another reason he was pleased his mother was now quite the silver surfer, even if his father refused flatly to go near the PC.

His fingers hovered over the keyboard as he tried to work out if he had a good excuse to duck out of travelling out of London to Folkstone next weekend. Eventually, he groaned and tapped out an acceptance.

He loved his parents, of course he did, but the house they'd owned for the last half century always seemed so bleak, despite the old-fashioned, over-cluttered décor. When he pictured that house in his mind's eye, nothing happened. No memories flooded his head. No jovial family dinners. No warm hugs to match the warm milk at bedtime.

His mother was one of those jolly-hockey-stick sorts who was much more likely to tell a child to pick himself up and stop making a fuss than kiss it better. But at least he saw a sparkle of warmth in her eyes occasionally. His father had been fossilised at birth.

Noah had thought that following him into the army might have elicited some longed-for approval. Noah had been wrong. The old man had hardly raised an eyebrow and had huffed something about how it would 'finally make a man of him'. His current success with his books produced only the odd snort, even though on one visit Noah had found one of his hardbacks hidden under his father's armchair with a corner folded down to keep his place.

He sighed. It didn't take one of his hunches to tell him that Grace wouldn't ration the affection and fun for her daughter, as if saving them for a rainy day that never came.

Finding that his hand had automatically returned to his mouse, he made use of it. There were a number of emails from Blinddatebrides.com and he clicked on one, wondering if one was from her.

Another match suggestion. He tried to get excited about the honey highlights and the perfect smile, about the capable-looking professional woman whose profile seemed to match his every require-ment for a wife. But, when he imagined her sitting across the table from him at dinner, she refused to look like her picture. Her hair darkened. Her smile became mischievous. One eyebrow arched high.

Oh, dear. He knew what this meant.

He'd learned long ago that he was the sort of person who had hunches. Not just run-of-the-mill inklings, but powerful, knock-the-breath-out-of-you hunches. It had started when he'd been a teenager and had always been able to guess the plot lines of all his favourite TV programmes. Even the fiendishly clever detective shows. Sometimes, with very little visible evidence, he just knew how things were going to turn out—in life and on the screen.

Over the years, he'd learned to follow his hunches, hone his skills. His agent told him his ability to create rich and twisting plots that surprised and satisfied was the main reason his books were so successful. Sometimes his hunches were so strong, so deep-seated, they dug in and refused to let go, even when those around him questioned his sanity. When his subconscious went all Rottweiler on him, there was normally a good reason for it. He just didn't always know what that reason was until much, much later.

And his inner Rottweiler had decided it liked the look of Grace Marlowe.

Frankly, he couldn't blame it.

That was it then. No point in fighting it. He could pretend to himself he would test the waters, see how things went, but if he was brutally honest he knew how this would all end. How it must end.

Grace Marlowe would be his blind-date bride.

Shaking his head at how sensible that sounded, how right he felt about it, he flicked down to the next email on the list and opened it up.

Englishcrumpet has sent you the following message:

Dear Noah,
Thank you for the lovely dinner and for the beautiful flowers. I'm sorry if I gave you the wrong impression, but I'm not interested in another date and I want to be clear about that.

*Right now, friendship is all I'm looking for
and all I can offer you.
Best wishes, Grace.*

Noah folded his arms and stared at Grace's message. This was going to make the whole 'getting married to Grace' thing interesting. He smiled to himself. He liked interesting.

Friendship? Well, he'd see about that.

Vinehurst had always been a picturesque corner of London, but it had suffered a difficult period recently, with the small shops like grocers, butchers, ironmongers going out of business as trade moved to the supermarkets and out-of-town retail parks. For a while, many of the little shops on the High Street had been empty, or taken over by cut-price operations selling electrical goods or cheap toys. But in the last ten years the area had undergone a regeneration, with many of the more affluent Londoners looking for more affordable housing away from central London's rocketing property prices.

Not surprising, as it had wonderful properties, from charming terraced cottages to grand Victorian villas. He'd seen the potential well before it had become fashionable. That was another hunch that had worked out for him. Friends had told him he was mad to buy the old manor house 'out in the middle of nowhere'. It was actually right on the edge of the city where it finally ran out of steam and let the fields and woodland remain undeveloped. Those same friends had moaned it was on the 'wrong' side of London. Why didn't he try Buckinghamshire? Or Gloucestershire? The right sort of people lived in Gloucestershire.

But he hadn't wanted to try Buckinghamshire. He'd had a 'feeling' about Vinehurst. It had excellent transport links to London, an airport nearby for light aircraft and his house had doubled in value in the four years since he'd bought it, thank you very much.

He stuffed his hands in his pockets and hunched into his collar as he walked up the street. A woman passing in the opposite direction caught his eye. She was young and pretty, with long blonde hair, and was pushing a toddler in a pushchair. But her undoubted prettiness wasn't what caused him to do a double take. It was the hothouse flower tucked behind her ear. Last night's rain had left dampness in the air and the wind was slicing its way up the street. He'd be surprised if the bloom didn't wilt in a matter of seconds.

He shook his head and carried on striding up the slight hill towards The Coffee Bean. No matter. People could do whatever they liked with their flowers. It didn't bother…

An old man with a flat cap nodded at him as they passed on the narrow pavement. Noah stopped in his tracks and swivelled round to look at him. In the buttonhole of his dirty grey overcoat was the most stunning orchid.

Something tickled at the back of his brain. There was a connection here. There had to be.

He was almost at the café now and, as he paused to let a couple of middle-aged women out of the door, he noticed they were also carrying a couple of exotic flowers each. What the…?

Once inside, he spotted Grace, sitting at a table close to the counter and carefully passing out flowers—his flowers—to every customer as they collected their drinks and wandered off to find a table.

He walked to the front of the queue and stood there, waiting for her to finish fiddling about with the remains of the bouquet he'd sent her. He knew the exact moment she sensed his presence because she went quite still.

Noah smoothed his face into the dictionary definition of 'calm and collected'.

Grace swore and jumped up.

'Noah! What are you…? I mean, why…?'

He blinked and nodded towards the foliage in front of her. 'More to the point, what are *you* doing?'

Grace bit her thumbnail. 'Sharing the love?' she said hopefully.

It was impossible to hold his mask of composure in the face of such genuine mortification. He smiled and Grace exhaled visibly.

She looked quite different from the night before—no dress, no heels, no clipped-up hairdo. Just jeans, a cute little wrap-around jumper in soft, soft blue and her hair swinging loose around her shoulders. She didn't look at all like the polished woman he'd imagined he'd end up with when he'd signed up to Blinddatebrides.com. She did, however, look completely adorable.

Grace stood up and hurriedly gathered the left-over bits of stalks and leaves into the tissue and cellophane on the table and threw them in a bin somewhere behind the counter. When she returned, she flicked her hair forward to cover her eyes.

'I sent you an email,' she said, twisting her thumb in the grip of her other hand.

'I know. I read it.'

Confusion clouded her features. 'Then why are you here? What do you want?'

Another one of those hunches slammed into him. If he pushed the issue now, she'd never agree to a second date. He knew that as certainly as he'd known the answer to three down on the crossword this morning. If he was going to find his perfect wife, he would have to plan this like one of his plots, set things up. He would need to be patient. Just as well he was very good at being patient when he'd set his mind on something.

'What I really want,' he said, watching her eyes

widen, 'is an espresso and a piece of that divine-looking chocolate torte.'

'Erm…okay.' Grace forgot entirely that she wasn't actually rostered to work that morning and skipped behind the counter to get Noah's coffee and cake. Caz was suspiciously silent and Grace felt her beady eyes on her as she carefully levered a slice of her famous torte onto a clean plate. She shoved the cake in his direction, holding the plate at arm's length.

'There you go. Take a seat.' She nodded at the half-empty café. 'I'll bring your coffee over when it's ready.'

She messed around at the coffee machine far longer than necessary. Why was he here? Didn't he believe her when she said she wasn't going to see him again? And how dared he look all sleek in his black jeans, his dark hair all wind-blown and sexy? It just wasn't fair that a man of his age should be twice as good-looking in the daylight.

When she'd done absolutely everything she could think of to delay giving Noah his coffee—save drinking it herself—she took a deep breath and walked over to where he was sitting. He'd chosen a slightly dilapidated floral armchair and, although she suspected that leather and clean lines were more his style, he looked totally at home in the higgledy-piggledy coffee shop.

'Here.' She placed the cup on the table to avoid

accidentally brushing fingers with him, then slumped into an adjacent chair.

'Well, that's me sorted,' he said, wrapping his long fingers around the little cup. 'Now, Grace Marlowe, what is it that you want?'

Grace had no idea.

But she did know what she *didn't* want. She didn't want to be sitting here noticing his fingers, because that led to noticing his wrists and the muscular forearms that were just visible where he'd pushed his sleeves up. How did a man have beautiful wrists? Just looking at them made her fizz inside. And fizzing led to something else she didn't want—doubting her decision to say no to a second date.

Slowly, she became aware that the ridge of her thumbnail was between her teeth and she pulled it away. Bad habit. She hooked the offending digit in the loop of her jeans and took a sudden interest in the glass display case on the other side of the room.

What did she want?

Better focus on that, because getting up and wandering off to choose something to eat would give her an excuse to avoid this awkward silence. She sneaked a look at Noah. He didn't seem to be finding it awkward at all. The torte was half-finished and he was sipping his coffee. If only she could match his serenity.

A croissant would be nice.

Something plain to settle her stomach. She pushed her weight down onto her feet and began to stand but, before she got fully vertical, a plate holding a pain au chocolat appeared before her.

'Thought you might need this,' Caz said and plonked a large black coffee down too. And then she sauntered off, looking as innocent as the day she was born. Grace knew better.

What Grace had *wanted* was to get away from Noah for a few moments, to allow her heart rate to return to normal, to get far enough away to block her view of his wrists. She definitely hadn't *needed* Caz's pain au chocolat—or her so-called help. Just as she hadn't needed to feel all heart-fluttery about Noah last night. It was a conspiracy.

'Grace? What do you want?' he said softly.

Grace poked her finger into her pastry, scooped up a chunk of brittle, bitter dark chocolate and sucked it off her finger. 'This'll do.'

Noah didn't display his fine teeth again, but she saw a glint of humour in his eyes. 'Not for breakfast. What do you want out of life?'

She pulled a face. 'That's a bit deep and philosophical for a Sunday morning, isn't it?'

He shook his head and loaded his fork with more torte. 'I'd say it was a perfect Sunday morning type of question.' She watched him in silence as he ate his cake, having no choice but to notice his fingers, his lips. He had very nice lips. And didn't she know how nice those lips could feel!

She deleted that thought. She couldn't feel that way again. Shouldn't be able to. That part of her soul had been a one-shot deal and she'd used it up on Rob.

'Okay then. Tell me about your daughter.'

That was easy. She knew what Daisy wanted. 'She's backpacking for a year before starting university up north. In fact, she's probably eating a very similar breakfast to mine in Paris, right this very second.'

Grace stared hard at her pain au chocolat, wishing it had magical powers and could transport her to a city with the best, most ostentatious patisseries in the world. What she wouldn't give to gaze in wonder upon shelves stacked high with gorgeous rainbow-coloured macaroons, tartes and choux buns.

'I wish I was in Paris too,' she whispered to herself, just for a moment forgetting the hunk of charm and cool sitting next to her.

'Well, that's an answer. Grace wants to travel.'

'Huh?' She looked up to find he had leaned in a little closer. What was he doing? Compiling a list?

'Now your nest is empty, you want to see the world?'

She nodded. 'That would be lovely, but I have to be content to just do it in my dreams. I'm…er…not really in a position to just jet off to some far-flung place on a whim.'

She took in the cut of Noah's coat, his effortless style. Everything about him screamed money. He obviously didn't have to worry about university fees or saving for his own little shop one day.

'This cake is fabulous,' he said before finishing the last mouthful.

There wasn't a smudge of chocolate on him. Not even a crumb had dared to land on his charcoal pullover. Grace licked a spot of stickiness off her fingers, then wiped them on her jeans.

'Who's your supplier?'

For a moment, Grace couldn't work out what he was asking. Then she blushed. The way she'd blushed at fourteen years old when she'd walked past The Coffee Bean and Rob had winked at her. The heat started in her neck and just kept on climbing.

'I am. I mean… I made it.'

For the first time since she'd met him—less than twenty-four hours ago, but it seemed a lot longer—Noah looked something other than cool. 'You did?'

She nodded, blushing hard enough now to match the icing on the finger buns in the display case.

'You have a real talent. Where did you learn to bake like this?'

Coming from Noah, a man who seemed to be a connoisseur of virtually everything, that meant something.

'I was at the end of a catering course at Westminster College when I had Daisy,' she said, looking at the crumbs on Noah's plate and wondering if you could read the patterns in the same way that gypsies read tea leaves. 'I had an idea I'd like to become a pastry chef.'

But long hours, early starts, the sheer hard graft that went along with working in a professional kitchen, had not been compatible with motherhood—especially single motherhood.

After Rob had died she'd been desperate. Twenty-year-old newlyweds didn't think about saving and life insurance. The army pension helped, but it had still been a struggle. Thank goodness Caz had come to her rescue. It had seemed like an answer to prayer. Not only had she had a roof over her head and a job, but a whole host of coffee shop employees virtually fighting each other to babysit Daisy. And she'd been able to bake. Okay, she hadn't finished her course, but she'd borrowed books from the library and even done a few adult education classes. At least working in The Coffee Bean had allowed her to indulge in her passion.

She bit into her pain au chocolat. The dark sweetness soothed her, as always.

'One day, I'm going to open my own patisserie,' she said quietly. She didn't know when or how, she just knew she would do it. But, instead of getting closer to her goal, her dream seemed to be disappearing into the distance like the retreating tide on the river Thames. And once the tide was gone, all that was left was mud. With every step, in every direction, she found herself stuck, held fast by the dark, sticky circumstances of life.

She looked up to find Noah regarding her, his grey-green eyes strangely intense. Suddenly, she realised there was another bullet point to add to the list of things she didn't want.

She didn't want to sit here feeling so comfortable in his presence that she drifted off, let her guard down, spilled her secrets at his feet.

'I have to go.' She stood up and jammed her hands into her jeans pockets. 'And I meant what I said, Noah. The flowers are lovely but—'

He reached up and tugged one hand out of her pocket. Just the feel of those long fingers wrapped around hers stole the words right out of her mouth. He tugged her down again and she sat with a bump.

'Don't look so scared, Grace,' he said and released her hand. 'I'm not about to stalk you, but I really enjoy spending time with you. If friendship is all you are offering, then I accept.'

Grace was speechless. That was what she'd said, but that wasn't what she'd meant. Not really. But as Noah slipped his long dark coat on, said his farewells and walked out of The Coffee Bean, she couldn't think of a single countermove. Automatically, she cleared his plate and walked over to the counter, where she handed it over to Caz. With nothing left to do in the café she opened the back door, navigated the narrow passageway there and climbed the stairs to her flat.

Down below, Caz stared hard at the dirty plate, twisting it this way and that in the light. And, when she was satisfied she'd looked long and hard enough, she smiled to herself and brushed the crumbs into the bin.

CHAPTER FOUR

GRACE smiled as she opened Noah's latest email. Once you got through that ever-smooth façade, he could be really insightful and funny. Finding a message from him in her inbox always brightened her day. And he'd been true to his word. In the last six weeks she hadn't felt stalked, not one little bit. She was glad of his friendship. She still missed Daisy like crazy but it was Noah, along with the girls from Blinddatebrides.com, who kept her going.

Grace smiled as she hit the 'send' button on her email. She'd thought she'd be horribly lonely without Daisy around but, after that day she'd stumbled into the chat room and sent out a distress call, she'd been in constant contact with Dani from San Francisco and Kangagirl, really Marissa from Sydney.

She wasn't quite sure what had caused them to bond so firmly. They had very different jobs and lifestyles, but they just 'got' each other. And having two neutral ears to share her dating worries with had been a godsend.

She flipped the laptop closed and padded off to the kitchen in search of a snack. There were another two hours to kill until her scheduled chat with Marissa and Dani at midnight. A strange time of day to get sociable but, considering that Marissa was thirteen hours ahead and Dani was eight hours behind, live chats had to take place at either midnight or six o'clock in the morning. And the girls knew how she felt about six o'clock in the morning.

It actually seemed a little bit sad that her best friends lived on different continents and she'd never met them face to face. She didn't know how they liked their coffee or what their voices sounded like, but maybe that was a good thing. Yes, there was a lot of banter, but when that died down they weren't afraid to be honest with each other. They'd got to know each other so much better over the Internet than if they'd met up and done small talk over coffee.

Sadder still had been the realisation that the greater part of Grace's socialising up until now had involved Daisy and a group of friends. They were cool kids, but she doubted they wanted a forty-year—a *mature* woman hanging around now Daisy was overseas.

Grace raided the biscuit barrel and sat down with a glass of milk at the kitchen table—a great little find from a junk shop. It was pure nineteen-fifties Americana, complete with chrome legs and trim and a speckled Formica top.

As Grace munched, she began to frown. She hardly ever just sat in her kitchen and had a really good look around. There was something about it. Something she just couldn't put her finger on. It reminded her of…

Oh, God. It reminded her of student accommodation.

Suddenly she was on her feet, walking through her flat looking at everything with unfettered eyes.

She realised with horror that her approach to decorating hadn't changed much since she'd married Rob. Oh, the colours and the prints and the bad flat-pack furniture had changed, but the essential philosophy—cheap, bright and fun—was exactly the same. Shouldn't there be at least one set of nesting tables in her living room? Where were the dinky ornaments, bought with a completely straight face and displayed with pride on the doily-topped mantle?

Okay, maybe she was taking this a bit too far, but Noah was her age and she'd bet he didn't have a stick of flat-pack furniture in his house. With relief, she reckoned he probably didn't have any doilies or nesting tables either, but she'd bet his place still looked…well…grown-up.

She turned into her bedroom and surveyed the turquoise and fuchsia Indian-inspired bedding. She loved it, loved the bright colours and sparkly embroidery, but nothing about it said 'mature and sophisticated'. Should it? Did she want it to?

She was standing next to the end of the bed and dropped onto it, staring at herself in a long mirror on the wall. They were more lines on her face than there had been twenty years ago—was that really all that had changed? When Daisy had been at home, all this noise and colour had seemed fun, had seemed right. Now, it jarred.

She was living in a time warp.

The urge to bury her face in her hands was irresistible, so she didn't bother to resist it. She was going to end up like Mrs Sims who came into The Coffee Bean, wasn't she? Mrs Sims, who at eighty still wore bobby socks, white plimsolls and a skirt that was just crying out to have a poodle appliquéd onto it.

She stood up and wandered into the living room and flicked the telly on. After channel surfing for a few minutes, she stopped at one of her all-time favourite movies—an eighties high school, coming-of-age flick. It didn't matter that she'd missed the first twenty minutes, she practically knew the lines by heart, anyway. It would fill the time nicely until her chat with Marissa and Dani and stop her thinking of poodles and figurines that were a nightmare to dust.

* * *

Blinddatebrides.com is running 12 chat rooms, 41 private IM conferences, and 4955 members are online.

Private Instant Messaging conference between Englishcrumpet, Sanfrandani and Kangagirl:

Englishcrumpet: Come on, Dani. Entertain us with your dating disasters! I can't ask Marissa because she's disgustingly about-to-be-wed and full of the joys of love.

Sanfrandani: Oh, you know…Same old, same old.

Englishcrumpet: But that's just it, Dani! We don't know. You're always so vague.

Kangagirl: It's time to spill the beans.

Englishcrumpet: Look, I told you about my dating bellyflop! Don't try and divert the conversation, Dani. Tell me you've had your fair share of no-hopers.

Sanfrandani: I've had my fair share of no-hopers.

Kangagirl: And…details, please?

Sanfrandani: And your one date wasn't a total washout, Grace. Has the mysterious Noah popped into the coffee shop any time recently?

Englishcrumpet: Yes, he has. In fact, he's got into the habit of appearing at The Coffee Bean pretty regularly—for coffee and something sweet, he says.

Kangagirl: Awwwww. What does he do again?

Not many men have time to lounge around in coffee shops in the middle of the day.

Englishcrumpet: He doesn't lounge—he brings his laptop and sits there alternately talking to himself, typing and staring into space. He writes stuff.

Sanfrandani: What kind of stuff?

Englishcrumpet: Oh, I don't know. Military stuff. Spy stuff.

Sanfrandani: And his name is Noah?

Englishcrumpet: Duh! Yes!

Sanfrandani: Have you looked for his stuff in a bookstore?

Englishcrumpet: No. Do you think I should?

Sanfrandani: Yeah, I really do.

Englishcrumpet: Anyway, that's irrelevant. I just want to stress (looking at no one in particular, Marissa) that Noah and I are just friends.

Kangagirl: Just good friends. Now where have I heard that before?

Englishcrumpet: We are good friends now. But I'm starved of girl-type gossip since Daisy's been gone. Come on, girls! Give me something juicy!

Sanfrandani: I might gossip a bit more if I could get a word in edgewise sometimes.

Englishcrumpet: Sorry! Look, you really don't have to talk if you don't want to, Dani. I realise some people aren't as happy to witter on about themselves as I am.

Kangagirl: Noah doesn't seem to mind.

Englishcrumpet: Seriously, Marissa, there's nothing going on. I know you want to believe that everyone is going to fall in love as quickly and completely as you did with Rick, but I'm not looking for that. I just like the fact that Noah doesn't see me as 'Daisy's mum'. I'm just Grace with him.

Kangagirl: You can't blame a girl for trying to matchmake.

Englishcrumpet: Wanna bet?

Englishcrumpet: Can I ask you girls something?

Sanfrandani: Sure.

Kangagirl: Go ahead.

Englishcrumpet: I'm not mutton dressed as lamb, am I?

Sanfrandani: Cookery questions? Is that some strange 'olde English' recipe?

Englishcrumpet: No, I mean…do I act too young?

Kangagirl: You're fun, Grace! Don't change that.

Sanfrandani: You know we love you just the way you are.

How did she explain this? It wasn't about being fun. It went deeper than that—in ways she didn't

really understand. In lieu of precise thinking, she
did the best she could:

> *Englishcrumpet: I know this sounds weird, but
> I think it's time for me to come of age.*

Noah tried to doze in his first-class seat, but there
was too much turbulence and, after five minutes of
nodding off then being jolted awake, he gave up and
asked a flight attendant for a coffee. When it arrived
he wished he hadn't bothered. It just made him
homesick for cobbled streets and wild flowers in
enamel jugs.

It made him think about Grace.

He seemed to be doing a lot of that recently. Especially when he was away from home. He missed
going into The Coffee Bean, missed the waft of
butter and cinnamon and ground coffee as he opened
the glazed front door and heard the bell jangle.

He and Grace had got into a routine when he
wasn't travelling. He would turn up at the café
around mid-morning, after he'd made a dent in his
word count goal for the day. It was a great incentive.
Suddenly, he was twice as prolific as he had previ-
ously been. Grace would just bring him an espresso
and whatever cake or muffin she thought he might
enjoy. They were always outstanding. He had no
doubts that she could have worked at any of the top
restaurants in London if she'd finished training.

While he privately lamented her missed opportunities, he also applauded her choices. She'd sacrificed all of that to bring up her daughter. There were many parents who just didn't get that. The more he knew Grace, the more he was certain his hunch about her was right. She was an amazing woman, possessing all the qualities he could want in a wife. And if he could gift-wrap a patisserie for her and deliver it to her doorstep, he would. She deserved it.

But he was just a friend. And friends didn't do that kind of thing.

He took another sip of the aeroplane coffee, grimaced and set it to one side. Might as well take his mind off the rest of the journey by sorting out chapter seventeen. Somehow it had gone off course, and the pace had slowed to zero. He opened up his laptop and took a quick look at his emails before he started working. A few had arrived while he'd been sitting in the terminal in Stuttgart and he hadn't had a chance to read them yet.

There was one from Grace, wishing him a nice time in Germany and recounting a funny Coffee Bean anecdote. He decided in that moment that, when he saw her next, he was going to pull her to one side and tell her who he really was. He trusted her completely. And she definitely wasn't out to marry him for his money. She wasn't out to marry him at all. What a pity.

The next email was a reminder from his agent.

Oh, hell. He'd forgotten all about that.

Next week was the British Book Awards and he'd get way too much stick if he didn't put in an appearance, especially as his latest cold war story had been shortlisted for Best Thriller. Too much of a PR opportunity for his publishers not to nag him senseless about it.

He'd been trawling Blinddatebrides.com for a suitable 'date-buddy', but he'd been so busy that he hadn't actually got past the looking-at-profiles stage. Which meant another ceremony which he would have to treat like a military operation if he was going to keep one step ahead of the glamour vixens. It was all so very tiring.

Could he schedule a date this week before the ceremony? And wasn't it a bit fast to ask someone he'd only just met to come with him? When he was his alter ego, Noah Smith, women were pleasant and interested, but they were hardly stalker material. What if, when he revealed his secret in a big *ta-dah* moment, his date turned all bunny-boiler on him? A week just wasn't long enough to test the waters.

His inner Rottweiler whined and barked.

Yes, yes, there was Grace. But she didn't want a relationship. She just wanted…

He didn't need a wife for next Thursday. He just needed a date. Someone to stand by his side, charm the socks off everyone and deflect the Mrs Frost wannabes.

Grace would be perfect. But would she do it? If he asked her nicely?

During her break, Grace took a journey next door to the book shop. She waved at the man behind the counter, who wore a home-knitted waistcoat every day of the year, even on a glorious April day like today.

'Morning, Martin. How are things going?'

Martin shook his head. 'What with all the posh shops opening up round here, the landlord wants to raise the rent. It's not right—all these newcomers pricing the locals out of business. I was only just surviving competing with all those online book-sellers as it was.'

'Will you fight it?'

The old man sighed. 'No point. The lease is up for renewal next month and I don't have the cash for all the solicitor's fees. If my son had wanted to take it on, I'd think about it, but it's only me now and my wife'll kill me if I don't retire in two years' time.'

A defiant look crossed Grace's face. 'Well, I'm spending all my book money here until you go, and I'm going to tell everyone who comes into the coffee shop to do the same. We'll give you a good send-off and a wodge of money for your retirement.'

Martin went a little red and pretended to attend to a stray thread in his waistcoat. 'Thanks, love. Now, what were you looking for?'

'Military history,' said Grace, feeling a little flutter in her tummy as the words left her mouth.

Now, where would Grace be on a fine morning like this, if she wasn't in The Coffee Bean? Noah peered through the window. Caz waved madly at him and motioned for him to come in.

She was a character in her own right, that one. Today, she was dressed head to foot in white and rhinestones, from her bejewelled flip-flops to her floaty skirt and the scarf in her hair. If she stepped outside into the sunshine, she was likely to blind someone.

He opened the door and wandered up to the counter, eyeing up the display case. There was a new pink thing in there, with raspberries and white chocolate, and he was itching to taste it. Who cared that he'd had to double the length of his morning runs to make sure his trousers didn't get too tight?

'She's just popped next door,' Caz said, not even pretending to beat around the bush.

Caz knew. Noah knew she knew. They both smiled at each other.

'Fine. Could I have a coffee and some of that raspberry thing while I'm waiting?'

Caz just winked at him.

* * *

Martin's military section was completely out of proportion to the size of his shop, Grace thought as she ran her index finger along the spines on yet another shelf. Mind you, he looked the sort to enjoy making up intricate model aircraft kits, so perhaps it was a passion.

She couldn't find a Noah Smith anywhere. But this was a little book shop on a small suburban high street. Perhaps she'd have to go further afield. Perhaps she'd have to use the Internet to find his titles, even if she ordered the actual book from Martin.

Two women walked into the shop as she emerged from behind the shelves and headed for Martin's counter.

'Have you got number four in the *Frozen Spies* series?' one asked. 'The latest is in the window, but my son has just got into them and wants to read them in order.'

'Let me go and look, madam,' Martin said and scurried off.

Madam. So quaint. And Grace would lay money on the fact that whatever franchise bought this little shop wouldn't have staff that said anything but, *Huh?*

'Did you see him on telly the other week—on that Friday night chat show?' the second woman said while she rummaged in her handbag for something.

'Who?'

'The author of *Frozen Spies*.' She nudged her friend and did a wink that didn't quite work. 'Wouldn't mind a little bit of undercover action with him myself, if you know what I mean.'

Grace stifled a smile as Martin returned with a book and placed it on the counter. 'Here we go! *Wasteland. Frozen Spies* number four.'

The book-buying woman picked it up and checked out the photo on the back as Martin rang it into the cash register—nothing so newfangled as a bar code scanner in this shop, thank you very much.

'Ooh, yes,' she said, winking at her friend. 'I see what you mean! Come to Mama!'

And the pair of them collapsed into giggles like a pair of fifteen-year-olds. Unfortunately, Martin's prehistoric till was playing up and it looked as if Grace would have a long wait if she wanted to quiz him about military books. She waved at him over the top of the giggling duo's heads and mouthed, 'I'll be back later.'

With a scone, probably. Martin looked as if he could do with a little cheering up.

Out of curiosity, she looked for the book the woman had been talking about as she walked past the window. There was a large display of a dramatic-looking hardback, the jacket in shades of silver and blue and grey.

Silent Tundra by Noah Frost.

Grace ran back into the shop and dived into the window display.

Noah choked on the raspberry thing when he saw Grace striding into The Coffee Bean with his latest book clasped in her hand. She spotted him sitting in his usual spot and he could have sworn he'd seen a wave of static electricity run up her body and leave her hair standing just a little on end.

Part of him was truly worried about what she was going to say; part of him was triumphant at this totally unique reaction to his identity.

'Oh! Mr *Smith*. So lovely to see you!'

He tried to swallow the mouthful of pink raspberry mousse stuff and just made himself cough again. Grace whacked him on the back. With the book. He really should try and write thinner ones.

He swallowed hard and managed to clear his mouth of food. His voice came out hoarse and raspy. 'Grace! I can explain…'

'I bet you can! But I don't want any more of your lies.'

'Grace—' the voice was low and authorative, and coming from the woman in white with her hands on her hips '—you are creating a scene in my coffee shop.'

Grace shut her mouth and looked around. Noah

counted at least twenty pairs of eyes staring at them. Not even a teaspoon clinked.

'Sorry, Caz.'

'Now, go and have a walk and calm down. Listen to what the man has to say.'

'I—'

'Go,' Caz said and nodded at the door.

Grace stalked out of the shop with the book tucked under her folded arms. Noah followed her. She waved his book at him. 'I have to give this back to Martin. I didn't pay for it.'

He just nodded and caught up with her. He could wait a few minutes if he got the chance to explain.

The book shop owner was standing in his doorway, frown lines furrowing his forehead. Noah nodded at him as Grace swept past him and climbed into the shop window. He, the shop owner and two customers watched in silence as she rebuilt a pyramid of books.

'Oh, my God, it's you! It's him, Julie!'

Noah closed his eyes and waited for the ground to open. Of all the times…

'Will you sign my book for me?'

Grace emerged from the window display and stood, arms folded across her chest next to the door. 'Yes, Noah. Why don't you sign the lady's book for her?'

He couldn't really do anything else, could he? The shop owner hurried round the other side of the counter and produced a pen. Noah took it from him and scribbled his standard best-wishes-hope-you-enjoy-the-book thing.

'Can you put "To Julie, with love"?'

Noah compromised and put "To Julie".

'I haven't got a book,' the other woman said. 'Could you sign something else for me?' She hunted around in her handbag as Noah handed Julie her signed copy.

'Aren't you tall,' Julie said, shuffling a little closer. 'Were you really a spy?'

'No,' Noah said, resisting the urge to clench his teeth. 'I make it up. It's fiction.'

'I bet no one's told you this before, but I reckon you'd make a fabulous James Bond.'

Actually, he'd heard that line so many times he couldn't count. Next she'd be telling him he looked like—

'You remind me a bit of Pierce Brosnan,' the other women chimed in.

Noah looked over at Grace, whom he expected was billowing smoke by now. She was just standing there, her arms by her sides, her quick eyes taking the whole situation in. That was it. He was never going to get any further with her now.

'I can't find a bit of paper,' Julie's friend said with a giggle. 'How about this?'

And she leaned forward and parted her blouse to reveal an expanse of crêpey décolletage. Noah dropped the pen. When he stood up, Grace handed him one of his hardbacks that she'd nabbed from the window display. Again.

'How about I just sign this one for you?' he said quickly and started writing before she had a chance to disagree.

'Don't worry, Martin,' Grace whispered to the man behind the counter. 'He's paying. Full whack too. None of this 'special offer' nonsense.'

Martin nodded and busied himself with a pot of rubber bands.

The two women left in a flurry of good wishes and 'hope to bump into you again's. Noah turned to look at Grace.

'Okay,' she said, her face unusually expression-less. 'I get it.'

Blinddatebrides.com is running 12 chat rooms, 27 private IM conferences, and 5212 members are online.

Englishcrumpet: You'll never believe what I've got to tell you about Noah! You know I said he was a writer?
Sanfrandani: Yes.
Englishcrumpet: Well, it turns out he's rather famous.
Sanfrandani: I knew it!
Englishcrumpet: Couldn't you have told me?
Sanfrandani: I wasn't sure. I just suspected.

Kangagirl: Hey, girls? Care to fill me in. I don't know anything about anything, it seems.

Englishcrumpet: Have you heard of Noah Frost?

Kangagirl: !!!!!!!!!!

Kangagirl: Really? That's him?

Sanfrandani: He's hot.

Englishcrumpet: Hands off, Dani!

Kangagirl: Thought you were just good friends, Grace.

Englishcrumpet: Sort of. We are. It's just…Oh, this is getting so complicated!

Sanfrandani: That's what we're here for, to help you out.

Kangagirl: Fill us in and we'll provide virtual hugs and real sympathy.

Englishcrumpet: He's got a big event to go to and he's asked me to go with him.

Kangagirl: I knew you two were more than JGF!

Englishcrumpet: JGF?

Kangagirl: Just Good Friends! You're always mentioning him.

Englishcrumpet: No, I'm not. And, anyway, I see him almost every day. It's not surprising his name pops into the conversation. And he was the very reason I found you two in the first place…

Sanfrandani: It's probably more accurate to say that you found us because of Daisy's prank.

Englishcrumpet: Same thing.

Kangagirl: Not exactly…

Sanfrandani: How is Daisy, anyway? Where is she now?

Englishcrumpet: I had an email from her yesterday. She's in Athens and doing fine. She had this really funny story about a goat and a moped…

Kangagirl: Don't think you're getting away without spilling the beans on your date with Noah! Hunky authors first, goats second!

Englishcrumpet: Honestly, Marissa! Are you this bossy in real life? Poor Rick!

Sanfrandani: Stop evading the issue, Grace. Are you saying that Blinddatebrides.com really did make a good match with you and Noah after all?

Englishcrumpet: We're just date-buddies. That's all.

Kangagirl: Deep down, I don't think you want to love again.

Englishcrumpet: Maybe you're right. I used to think I couldn't love anyone the way that I loved Rob. And part of me still thinks that's true.

Sanfrandani: That's sad, Grace.

Kangagirl: But very sweet.

Englishcrumpet: But recently I've been thinking that I could find a nice man to share things with, but it'll be different. It won't be the same all-consuming thing I felt for Rob. It'll be gentler, calmer.

Sanfrandani: Sounds like you mean safer.

Englishcrumpet: Is love ever safe?

Kangagirl: Are you sure you can't find this gentler, safer love with Noah?

Sanfrandani: Grace?

Englishcrumpet: Stop already with the matchmaking! I'm going before you both attempt to brainwash me. Catch you later!

Kangagirl: Have a great date! Take care!

Sanfrandani: Bye!

Englishcrumpet has left the conversation.

Kangagirl: Hey, Dani? Do you think I'm barking up the wrong tree here? About Grace and Noah?

Sanfrandani: Don't know, Marissa. You're right—she does mention him a lot.

Kangagirl: Guess we'll just have to wait and see!

Sanfrandani: LOL. You're incorrigible, Miss Bride-to-be!

Sanfrandani: And wipe that goofy smile off your face.

Kangagirl: Busted! How did you know?

CHAPTER FIVE

GRACE let out a shaky breath as the car Noah had ordered for them drew up outside the Regent Palace, one of London's swankiest hotels. She turned to Noah.

'Are you sure about this? About me?'

He gave her a look that made her insides melt. 'Of course I'm sure.'

Right. Okay, then. Part of her had been hoping he'd slap his forehead and mutter, *What was I thinking?* She was just going to have to go through with it now.

'Grace?'

'Mm-hmm?'

'Relax. You look stunning.'

She gave him the tiniest of smiles. She'd dipped into her savings and bought a cocktail dress that she'd fallen in love with when walking past one of the exclusive little boutiques that had opened up in the High Street in the last couple of years. The fabric was the most amazing silver-grey silk and the dress had a fifties feel about it, with its wide, scooping

Audrey Hepburn neck and a soft, full chiffon skirt. It was looking a little creased after the car journey and she smoothed the ridges away with her palms.

Noah was looking pretty stunning himself. She totally agreed with the mad shopping lady's James Bond comparison, although she didn't think he looked like Pierce Brosnan at all. He had dark hair and matching charisma, but facially they were totally different.

The driver opened the door on her side. She looked down at her legs, wondering if she could remember the way to get out of a car in a dress without showing her knickers. It was something to do with keeping her knees together—or should it be her ankles? She scanned his face carefully as she took his hand and swivelled out of the car. His expression didn't change in the slightest and she thanked heaven that she must have got the manoeuvre right after all.

As she walked onto the red carpet, she felt like a trespasser, her strappy high sandals making little pock marks in the pile. Noah's strong hand clasped hers and tugged her into his side. Grace pulled herself straight and prepared herself to walk without making an idiot of herself.

While the event wasn't in the league of the film premieres in Leicester Square, there was a smattering of photographers and journalists and a small crowd had gathered. Noah walked over to the railing and shook hands and signed a couple of autograph books, all the time making sure she was by his side. People stared at her.

She tried to smile, but it felt so unnatural. A little muscle at the corner of one of her eyes kept twitching.

Oh, Lord. What was she doing here?

She was just a spare part. Window dressing. All fluff and no substance.

Noah signed the last autograph and slid his hand back into hers. She grasped it greedily and he leaned across to whisper something in her ear.

'You have no idea how much I hate this bit. I always feel such a fraud.'

They smiled at each other, just for a few seconds, before moving on.

Grace tried to ignore the crowd, the paparazzi, the fans pushing themselves at the barriers hoping to see a TV star or two. The women, both on and off the red carpet, were looking at Noah as if they'd like to serve him up for supper on a bed of chocolate, garnished with a sprig of mint in his belly button.

If there was anyone fake here, it wasn't him. She'd sneaked into Martin's book shop during the week and bought his first book. It had left her yawning—not because it was bad; far from it! She'd been yawning because she'd stayed up to two in the morning three nights in a row, totally caught up in the clever plot and life-and-death situations. It had left her feeling as if she had discovered a whole extra level to him.

Just a few days ago he'd been Noah Smith, the

nice-looking man who came into her café and ate cake. Now he was Noah Frost, the celebrity author, general superstar and stud-muffin. Suddenly, she was a little in awe of him.

He gently tugged on her hand and they were moving again, towards the liveried doormen who were guarding the hotel's front entrance. Grace let him pull her forwards and soon she was carefully placing her sandals on each step of a sweeping staircase, heading for the ballroom where the awards ceremony was being held.

When they reached the threshold to the room, Grace stopped, her eyes wide.

It was like something out of a fairy tale. A very modern fairy tale with glitz and glamour and celebrities instead of kings and nobles. She could see a few TV comedians and a couple of newsreaders just from where she was standing.

Huge marble columns lined the room and vast crystal chandeliers dripped from every part of the ornate plaster ceiling. Flowers were everywhere— enough to give the population of Vinehurst button-holes three times over.

Wow.

Noah squeezed her hand and she looked up at him. The smile for the cameras was gone now and his beautiful pale green eyes held such honesty. Her heart did a little pirouette.

'Thank you, Grace,' he said and placed a delicate

kiss on her cheek, just in front of her ear. 'I really appreciate you doing this for me.'

Was he kidding? Most women would sell their own shoe collections to be at an event like this, with a man like him. She straightened her spine. She would just have to think of good old Audrey in *My Fair Lady*—without the OTT cut glass accent, of course—and she'd be fine.

It struck her that this was New Grace's first public outing, her 'coming out' ball, if you liked. She squeezed his hand in return.

'Okay, Mr Frost,' she said, winking her mascara-laden eyelashes at him. 'Let's go get 'em!'

'Sorry you didn't get the gong, Noah.'

Noah turned to find one of the other authors from his publishing house standing beside him. Rebecca was the hot new thing in women's fiction at the moment and had won the award for Best Newcomer.

'Ah, you can't get too worked up about these things, can you?' He nodded at Rebecca's award, which she was clutching with one hand while she balanced a glass of champagne in the other. 'Congratulations to you, though.'

'Thanks.' She sipped her drink for a moment and looked across the room.

'And are congratulations supposed to be coming in your direction too?'

Noah laughed. 'Not unless I go and "relieve" Frankie of his award and run very fast indeed.'

Rebecca rolled her eyes. 'Not the award, dummy. Her.' She gestured in Grace's direction with her glass. The liquid sloshed around and glinted under the chandeliers. Rebecca focused on it slowly and then took another glug.

'Grace?'

'There's much crying in the Ladies tonight, now everyone thinks you might be off the market.'

Noah tried to remain the picture of composure. 'And why would they think I might be "off the market" as you so eloquently put it?'

Rebecca licked her lips, blinked and swayed slightly. ''Cos you've hardly taken your eyes off her all evening. She must be pretty amazing if she's finally caught the attention of publishing's most eligible bachelor.'

Noah opened his mouth to pooh-pooh the whole 'eligible bachelor' thing, but suddenly the group around Grace erupted into laughter and he got caught up in watching her smiling and talking. 'She is pretty amazing, isn't she?'

Rebecca, however, was downing the rest of her glass and had obviously lost track of what they were talking about. 'I think it's time I held off the champers, Noah me old darling,' she said and let out a tiny burp.

'I think you're right, Becca.'

Noah ushered her in the direction of the lobby, where she said her boyfriend was waiting for her.

Once he'd safely handed her over, he went looking for Grace. They'd got separated a while ago and every time he tried to reach her, someone—

'Noah, me old mate!'

Here we go again, he thought, as he fixed a smile on his face and turned round. He stood chatting to the group for a while, but after the first ten minutes he found it easy enough to just sip his drink and nod. At literary parties, you were never short of someone who was ready to hold court. It just so happened that, this time, it was coming in rather handy.

Noah stood back and just watched Grace sparkle. She was talking to a group from his publishers and they were hanging on her every word. He was so glad she wasn't a carbon copy of everybody else here, that he had gone with his gut instinct.

He exhaled. There was only so much watching from the sidelines that a man could do. He extracted himself from the conversation he'd been having on autopilot and made a beeline for Grace. When he reached her side, he stood close and wrapped an arm around her waist. She didn't flinch. She didn't even scowl. She just finished what she was saying and flicked a glance in his direction, smiling. That smile was his undoing.

It wasn't one of her sassy smiles, or even one of her wide grins. This smile was soft, almost…shy.

His inner Rottweiler, who'd been sleeping nicely all evening, suddenly decided to go in for the kill.

He didn't want to look for anyone else. He didn't want to spend any more time scouring Blinddatebrides.com. He wanted Grace. He wanted to marry her.

As Noah handed Grace her coat, she sighed. 'What a great night!'

'I'm glad you enjoyed yourself.'

She gave him a look of sheer disbelief. 'Enjoyed myself? Did you see him? That guy who was in the latest Sunday night costume drama on telly? He kissed my hand. Twice!'

And Noah would like to punch him. Just once.

Grace put her hand over her mouth to smother a yawn. 'I'm so glad you decided to book hotel rooms for tonight.' It had been one of the sweeteners he'd come up with when trying to persuade her that this was a good idea. 'My feet are killing me and I couldn't face the drive back, not at—oh, my goodness! Is that really the time?'

He nodded. 'Cinderella left quite some time ago.'

She yawned again and set him off.

'Come on, Sleeping Beauty. Time to get a cab. The hotel we're going to is a little bit quieter than this one, thank goodness.'

'And I've got my own room?'

'Yes, for the third time tonight, you've got your own room! What do you think I am?'

* * *

The limousine nipped down side streets and darted round corners until Grace was hopelessly disoriented. She yawned again. She'd drunk just enough champagne to leave her feeling slightly fuzzy. Only about three glasses over the course of the evening, but she didn't get the opportunity to drink anything but cheap plonk from the local supermarket, and the real thing had gone straight to her head.

A head that was feeling rather heavy at present. And there was a nice warm chest close by, perfect to loll against.

The car swung round another corner and Grace let gravity take the blame as she landed on Noah. He didn't seem to mind, prising his arm from his side and resting it round her shoulders. A delicious bubbly feeling, which had nothing to do with champagne, started in her toes and worked its way up to her ear lobes.

She breathed out, long and steady. This was nice, leaning against Noah, feeling the warmth of his chest against her back and the pads of his fingers lightly brushing her upper arm. He smelled so good…

But they were here as friends, and it really wouldn't do to turn her head and bury her face in his shirt as she was tempted to do.

The sounds of hooting horns, revving engines and sirens were just starting to come from far, far away when the car stopped and Grace found herself being gently shaken. Everything seemed slightly unreal as she yawned and walked and yawned and walked, following Noah into lifts and along corridors.

A bellboy opened the door and she just stared at a fabulous room, all in cream and gold and ivory.

'There's no bed,' she said, frowning slightly. 'A room this nice and there's no bed?'

Noah put an arm around her back and ushered her into the room. 'It's a suite. Your room is this way.'

Grace didn't notice much about the room but the vast, squashy-looking bed. She twisted herself around and just fell onto it, her feet lifting off the floor with the force of impact. Heaven. If she could live in this bed for the rest of her life, she would.

Her shoes were being taken off and she wiggled her toes and let out a giant sigh that grew and stretched until it became yet another yawn. A pair of warm lips kissed her temple.

'Goodnight, Grace. Sweet dreams.'

Grace woke from a delicious sleep and stretched, long and hard, right down to the muscles in her toes and right up to the fingertips above her head. She was naked, having peeled off her dress some time in the night and climbed under the covers.

The clock by the bed showed it was eight. A fairly respectable time to rise after such a late night. She snuggled back into the goosedown pillow. It all seemed so decadent, lying in—on Egyptian cotton, no less—and not going into work today.

She had one last stretch and headed for the shower. When she'd finished, she pulled her pyjamas from her bag, which had miraculously appeared in her room, and then wrapped the soft white towelling robe from the back of the door over the top. She opened the door to the sitting room part of the suite and peered out. Noah was sitting at a desk near the window, working away on his laptop and looking as if he'd been conscious for hours.

He finished a series of taps, hit the enter key, then turned in her direction. 'Good morning. How did you sleep?'

Grace stepped into the room. 'Wonderfully, thank you…And thank you for such a great night last ni—oh, bother!' She pulled up the sleeve of her bathrobe and inspected her right hand. 'I wasn't going to wash the hand that Randolph Marks kissed, but I forgot all about that and gave it a good scrub in the shower.'

'Too bad,' Noah said, a smug smile twitching at his lips. 'How about some breakfast?'

He motioned to an open set of French windows and Grace gasped. Outside, on a small terrace that she hadn't even known existed, was a table laden with rolls and croissants, orange juice and fresh fruit platters.

She ran outside to look at it all. And then she leaned over the balcony. They were at least ten storeys up, and big red buses, taxis and cyclists all jostled far away on the street below. People in dark suits carrying briefcases hurried in straight lines. It was a beautiful morning, with the sky so blue it was almost too perfect. The trees lining the street below shimmered in the breeze and the sun was warm on her face and bare feet.

She sat in one of the wrought iron chairs circling the table, her bottom welcomed by a cushion at least five inches thick.

'This looks fabulous! Thank you so much, Noah—for all of this, last night… I feel like I'm on holiday!'

Noah joined her at the table and poured them both cups of coffee from the silver pot.

'No. Thank *you*. Your presence was very effective in keeping the undesirables at bay. I didn't get asked to autograph a cleavage once last night, so I count it a success.'

Grace grinned at him and reached for a croissant and loaded her plate with strawberries, raspberries and blueberries. 'You're welcome.' She broke off a piece of croissant and popped it in her mouth.

Oh, my. She'd died and gone to heaven. It was light, flaky and buttery all at the same time. As she rested in her chair, she idly thought about infiltrating the kitchens to see how the chef did it.

Breakfast was long and leisurely, with gentle banter and plentiful cups of coffee. When Grace was confident she wouldn't need to eat another thing until at least next Thursday, she propped her feet up on one of the spare chairs, closed her eyes and raised her face to the sun.

'I could get used to this.'

Off in the distance, the traffic roared and the wind lifted the fine hair at the edge of her temples. She sighed.

'Could you? Why don't you, then?'

Grace turned her head and lifted one eyelid. Noah was leaning forward, his chin on one of his fists, giving her a very serious look. A sudden shiver ran up her spine and she tugged her robe tighter around her. 'What do you mean?'

'I mean…'

Grace dropped her feet to the floor and sat up straight. Noah gulped in a breath, not looking at all like a sexy spy for once.

'I mean, you could live like this all the time… if you married me.'

A sudden wave of vertigo hit her. A delayed reaction from hanging over the balcony, probably.

'What did you just say?'

Noah stood up, circled the table and sat down in the chair she had just had her feet on. He took one of her hands in his and looked into her eyes.

'Marry me, Grace?'

The first time in her life, Grace didn't have a witty comeback, a smart reply. 'But…but…we're just friends…you don't love me.'

'I think you're wonderful, Grace. I have a great deal of respect for you. And I have fun when I'm with you. Fun I'd forgotten how to have.'

'But…'

'And there's plenty of chemistry between us.'

She looked down at their intertwined fingers, then back up at Noah. 'Yes, there is…' A little too much chemistry on occasion. 'But…'

'You said yourself that you weren't looking for Romeo and Juliet. I'm proposing a partnership based on the mutual respect, compatibility—' a small smile kicked the corners of his mouth up '—chemistry…'

Suddenly, he leaned in. She could feel his breath on her lips and, without warning, her heart rate doubled and her eyes slid closed. The kiss that followed was as soft and slow and balmy as the spring sunshine.

Noah pulled back and held her face in his hands, his eyes searching hers, asking questions, finding answers.

She'd missed this.

Not just the kissing—although it was pretty spectacular—but connecting with someone. She knew Noah was telling the truth. They *were* compatible. And he'd meant what he'd said, how he felt about her. No one had said those kinds of things about her for a very long time. Tears clogged the back of her throat.

But it wasn't love.

Could she agree to a marriage on the foundations

that Noah had outlined? A couple of months ago she'd have laughed herself silly at the idea, but now…

No more lonely days. No more struggling to do everything on her own. Someone to talk to when she was down. Someone to laugh with when she was happy. Suddenly her soul ached for those things.

She pulled away from him and stood up, pressing trembling fingers to her lips.

'I… I don't know, Noah. I need to think about this. I'd like to go home, please.'

Her heart was pounding so fast that Grace considered collapsing onto the top step and resting against the front door to her flat for a moment before she went inside. In fact, that was a fabulous idea. She turned and slumped against the door, letting gravity pull her into an untidy heap on the landing.

The ride home had been excruciating. She just hadn't known what to say. How could she have chit-chatted after a proposal of marriage? A proposal she hadn't actually turned down. Was she mad?

When the car had pulled up in the alley behind The Coffee Bean, where the back entrance to her flat was, she'd grabbed her overnight bag and bolted. And now she was sitting here, her heart rate returning to normal, and she still didn't know what to do.

Her flat was her space, her sanctuary, but she had absolutely no desire to go inside at the moment. The first thing that would greet her when she opened the door would be the photo of Rob in his uniform, holding Daisy just a few days after she'd been born.

She sighed. When they'd married, she and Rob had felt so grown up. And yet, when she looked back at her photo albums now, they both looked impossibly young, little more than children themselves. For goodness' sake, Daisy was almost the same age as Grace had been when she'd got married. Just the thought of Daisy with a ring on her finger and a bump under her T-shirt was enough to make Grace break out in a cold sweat.

Back then, she and Rob had been so convinced that what they had would last for ever, but what *really* would have happened if he'd still been alive? Would they have been the perfect family of her daydreams, or would they be living in separate houses, fighting over custody arrangements and child support?

How could she walk past that picture of Rob when she was thinking like this? She couldn't block him out and pretend he'd never existed, not when she'd spent all these years keeping him alive by being the Grace he'd fallen in love with.

She'd never doubted any of this before, not even in her twenties, when she'd dated quite a bit and had still been full of hope that she'd find someone new to fill the void in her life. But none of them had measured up to fun-loving, generous Rob, and twenty-something men had a habit of running scared from a ready-made family.

It had just confirmed what she'd known all along—Rob had been her soulmate and she wasn't going to find another man like him. Just wasn't going to happen. So she'd given up the search.

But now she'd found Noah.

He was nothing like her darling Rob, and any relationship she embarked upon with him would be totally different from her marriage. Noah wanted companionship, a partnership built on mutual respect. Those criteria hadn't even been on her radar when she'd accepted Rob's proposal. It had been about love and destiny and forever. Only forever hadn't come. And now she had to decide what to do with the time she had left, rather than treading water and pretending she had an endless supply of days left to her.

Respect. Compatibility. Support.

It all sounded so logical. Yet the Grace inside her who liked fishnets, tequila and rock concerts was yelling *no* and shaking her head. Was she just being childish?

Grace rubbed her hands over her face.

The scary thing was, part of her wanted to say yes. Part of her wanted all those things. And, if she decided she could move towards this idea of a more mature, balanced view of love, what did that mean for her marriage to Rob? Would she be crossing it out and saying it was a mistake?

She might not know what it meant, but it *felt* like betrayal.

On the other hand, that love-song, only-in-movies kind of thing wasn't the only kind of love. And perhaps, if that was what Noah wanted from her, she would have turned him down flat anyway. Love like that meant one thing—loss. It was as if the universe had to balance out the intensity by taking it away again. Too much perfection could not be good for a soul. And she couldn't survive that again, losing the man she totally adored.

So, on reflection, maybe Noah's idea was the logical choice…

Oh, she was going round in circles!

She sighed, stood up and let herself into the flat, avoiding both the photo and the laptop sitting on the coffee table in the living room. She had no intention of logging in to Blinddatebrides.com tonight to see if Marissa and Dani were hanging out there. They'd want to know about the so-called date.

She needed time to get her head round this before she shared it with anyone. She wasn't even going to tell Daisy yet.

* * *

Noah didn't come to The Coffee Bean for a few days, although he sent her a couple of very neutral emails in the meantime. He was such a gentleman, giving her space, knowing she'd freaked out a little. It was such a relief that she didn't have to explain it all to him, that he understood.

She could do a lot worse than Noah Frost.

Grace unpacked a batch of miniature chocolate tarts and pressed a single fresh raspberry into the smooth surface of each one before lining them up in the display case.

Caz would know what to do. She'd been like a surrogate mother to Grace and a surrogate grandmother to Daisy in the last couple of decades. Grace didn't go to her for advice often. Normally, because she didn't like the advice she got and, even more frustrating, it usually turned out to be spot-on.

But as she approached Caz, who was sitting in the corner table poring over a large accounts ledger, she realised that the older woman was staring off into space, not even looking at the web of figures on the page before her. It was the third time today Grace had spotted her doing this, and it just wasn't like her. She was normally so down-to-earth.

She pulled out an old wooden church chair— complete with hymn book holder on the back—and sat down opposite Caz.

'Penny for them?'

Caz sighed. 'I'm not sure they're worth it, but a couple of thousand might be more welcome.'

'Problems?'

Caz nodded and twisted the book round for Grace to have a look. Maths had never been her strong suit, unless it involved pounds and ounces rather than pounds and pence, and Grace was forced to nod without really knowing what she was looking at. She stood up again, walked behind Caz's chair and wrapped her arms around her shoulders, pressing her cheek against the side of Caz's face.

'Don't give up. We'll make it. We've always managed before.'

Caz just patted Grace's arm and stared off into the distance.

Private IM chat between Englishcrumpet, Kangagirl and Sanfrandani:

Englishcrumpet: Okay, girls. I have something to confess.
Kangagirl: Ooh! Juicy!
Sanfrandani: Ready and waiting.

Grace took a deep breath. She'd kept this info to herself for a few days, but now she needed to let it out.

Englishcrumpet: The day after we went to the awards, the date-that-wasn't-a-date? Well, Noah kissed me.

Kangagirl: !!!!!!!!!
Sanfrandani: Wow!
Englishcrumpet: I know.
Sanfrandani: This would explain why, after a severe case of mentionitis *where the author is concerned, you've suddenly gone quiet about him.*
Kangagirl: Grace? Why didn't you tell us before?
Sanfrandani: I can understand the need for a little privacy. Sometimes there are things you just need to keep to yourself. It's not a reflection on our friendship that Grace wouldn't— or couldn't—tell us. Right, Grace?
Englishcrumpet: Right! You know I think the world of you two! You're my sanity in an increasingly crazy existence. I just…couldn't get my head round it.
Kangagirl: So…how was it?
Englishcrumpet: It was…

She bit her lip. *Soul-churning? Firework-inducing? Utterly fabulous?*

Englishcrumpet: It was nice. Different from last time.
Sanfrandani: Grace!
Kangagirl: Last time!!!!!!!! Grace?
Englishcrumpet: Go easy on the !!!, Marissa. You're going to wear your keyboard out.

Kangagirl: (raspberry)
Sanfrandani: I'm guessing that, in your very British, understated way, that you're saying it was pretty great?

Grace covered her face with her hands. Even now, just thinking about the hotel terrace, she went all hot and tingly. She'd never be able to look at a croissant the same way again.

Kangagirl: And last time*!*
Englishcrumpet: Whoops! Forgot to mention that, didn't I? We had a little kiss after the first date.
Kangagirl: Little kiss? Grace, you're holding back. I can tell.
Englishcrumpet: Okay! Okay! He pressed me up against the coffee shop window and kissed me until I was left breathless and melting, is that what you want to hear?
Kangagirl: (grin) It's a start!

Grace chuckled, despite herself. Marissa was right. She *had* been holding back from her friends. Which was incredibly daft. She really needed someone to talk to at the moment. Her head was constantly going round in circles and sleep deprivation was setting in.

Sanfrandani: And you said no to a second date? Why?
Englishcrumpet: I was scared.

She hesitated for a moment, then began typing again.

Englishcrumpet: I still am.
Sanfrandani: What's happening now? Are you dating?
Englishcrumpet: Not exactly.
Sanfrandani: What does that mean?
Englishcrumpet: It gets worse.
Sanfrandani: How?

How did she say this? How did she explain all the weird things she'd been thinking, all the strange things that had been happening to her since that night? Did she tell them how her stomach did the high jump every time Noah walked in the coffee shop? Did she tell them about how, when she was alone in bed at night, she longed for him to be there with her, holding her, touching her…

She swallowed. Okay, she might not be ready to voice those thoughts, but there was something concrete she hadn't told them yet.

Englishcrumpet: He asked me to marry him.

* * *

For the first time in their Internet friendship there were no witty replies or strings of exclamation marks, no probing questions. These girls kept her real, asking the questions she was too scared to ask herself, encouraging her to reach beyond what she thought were her limits. But, right now, they were obviously just as stunned as she was about what she'd just told them.

After dealing with two very shocked friends, Grace logged off Blinddatebrides.com and turned off the laptop. Her brain was whirring far too hard to let her sleep, so she walked over to the bookcase and pulled out one of the photo albums.

Not the wedding one. One of the family ones, full of shots of her and Rob—and later Daisy too. A record of their relationship.

It had all seemed so romantic, marrying a handsome young soldier before he went off on active duty, and he'd come safely home again. That time.

She sighed. Rob had been husband material from the day he was born—kind, dependable, full of determination. Only a fool wouldn't have snapped him up the minute she'd laid eyes on him.

She flicked through the pages…She and Rob hanging out with their friends…The pair of them in front of the Christmas tree with matching Santa hats and silly grins. And then she came to her favourite one. The one she'd taken on their budget honeymoon in Broadstairs—Rob smiling at her as he sat on a wall eating fish and chips.

She almost couldn't bear to look at it.

Even though I haven't said 'yes' to Noah, I feel like I'm leaving you behind. How can I do that after all we were to each other?

She searched his smiling eyes, looking for answers.

Slowly, surely, the words filled her head, just as if he'd been sitting on the sofa with her with his arm round her, speaking to her, stroking the wisps of hair above her ears with his thumb. She knew exactly what Rob would have told her, his generous spirit and common sense shining through.

You have to. You have to leave me behind. You can't freeze-frame yourself and pretend that time hasn't moved on, because it has. A part of me will always be with you, but it's time to let go. Time to become who and what you were always supposed to be.

But did that mean accepting Noah or turning him down? And what was she supposed to be when she grew up, anyway? She gently closed the album and put it back on the shelf. At forty years and three months, she supposed it was high time she found out.

CHAPTER SIX

NOAH highlighted the last three pages he'd typed into his word processing program and hit the delete key with force. Then he highlighted the three pages before that and deleted them too.

His current hero was giving him hell and, no matter which way he tried to write him, he just wasn't working. Something just wasn't clicking.

He pushed himself away from his desk and let his chair roll backwards. What he needed was a change of scenery, a change of atmosphere. What he really needed was to stop thinking about Grace and what answer she'd give him. He didn't want to pressurise her, but the waiting was driving him crazy.

Maybe it would have been better if he'd picked a glamour vixen instead. At least he'd have had an unequivocal answer there and then.

Actually, he needed to walk. It was a great way to clear his head and get the ideas flowing. And if he could walk where other people were, even stop and watch them sometimes, so much the better.

Little questions popped into his head as he observed them, and these little questions were often the sparks for some of his best ideas.

Why is that guy wearing a coat in July? What are those two people sitting on the bench *not* saying to each other? Those sorts of things.

He got into his car and drove into Vinehurst and parked near the large common with a swing park at one end. Although the average person wouldn't think a bit of wild grassland was a great place to people-watch for a writer of spy novels, they'd be wrong. He often wrote about characters who looked so domestic, so benign on the surface, but underneath they were sinister, heroic or just plain nasty.

He stuffed his hands in his pockets and moved his feet. It was time to let his brain off the leash and see where it would run.

It was nearing six o'clock in the evening and most of the mums and kids had gone home for tea, leaving the common to dog-walkers and joggers, but as he passed the playground he spotted a lone figure, pushing themself backwards and forwards with a listless movement of one toe.

Why? his brain asked. Why is that person—an adult—sitting here all alone as the sun lowers in the sky? Why are they using one foot, not two?

He looked again, capturing the exact pose, the exact movement of the swing, because he knew this image was going to come in handy some day. But, as he looked again, he realised it was Grace sitting there on the swing and, suddenly, it stopped being an exercise in logic and became urgently personal.

'Grace?'

She almost jumped off the swing she was so surprised to hear his voice. She couldn't disguise the look on her face that said: *Oh, heck. Does it have to be him who finds me like this?* And then he noticed the puffy red patches under her eyes and the way she sniffed quietly, hoping he wouldn't notice.

'What's the matter?'

'Long story,' she said, finally giving in to a good loud blow into a tissue. He sat down on the vacant swing and they both stared out into the distance, rocking in time.

'Good job I like stories,' he said, risking a look at her. She looked back, but didn't smile.

'The Coffee Bean is on its last legs.' Her voice was almost monotone, so unlike her usual animated conversation. 'Java Express has made Caz an offer to buy the shop and I don't think she can afford to refuse it. If she waits until she has to sell, or goes bust, she won't get nearly as much.'

'You'll lose your job,' he said. 'What will you do?'

Grace sighed. 'I would go back to college and finish my training if I could, but I need a roof over my head. I need to work. Actually, I literally need a roof over my head. The flat is part of the deal.'

She shook her head and big fat tears rolled down

her cheeks. 'I can't stand the idea that they'll rip out that beautiful counter and pull up the floor. The Coffee Bean will lose all its character. They'll just make it…generic.'

Oh, hell. He never knew what to do when people cried. Really cried. He never let himself do it, so he couldn't even mimic what other people did when he was in the same situation. He didn't do huggy stuff and there-theres. Didn't know how.

What did Grace like? What would make her feel better?

Food.

Grace liked cooking. And she certainly enjoyed eating.

'Come on,' he said. 'I'm taking you to dinner.' He wondered if Barruci's would have a table free.

Grace looked up at him, her eyes hollow. He was about to pull his mobile phone out of his pocket and make a reservation when his inner Rottweiler growled at him. She stood, and didn't even bother trying to argue with him.

'Where are we going?'

'The Mandarin Moon.'

He didn't know why. He just knew it was the right choice.

Grace poked at her roast pork chow mein with a chopstick. She must really be in a bad way, Noah thought, if she couldn't polish this lot off. He offered her some more sweet and sour chicken and she just curled her lip.

'What are your options?' he said, putting the bowl back down on the table.

'I don't seem to have many options. I do okay working for Caz, but going to one of the large coffee shop chains would earn me virtually nothing. I'd have to move out of the area to find somewhere to live. But where the property is cheaper, the jobs are scarcer. Vicious circle.'

'And there's nothing you can do to save The Coffee Bean?'

She shook her head. 'Nope. I offered Caz my savings, but she said it would just be a drop in the ocean. It's a sad day when ten grand is a drop in the ocean.'

Ten grand. Not a lot to him, but Grace must have worked really hard to save that amount of money. Every day he knew her, there was more to marvel about her.

'In a month's time, I'll have no job, no home. No Daisy, even. It's worse than being back at square one. It's square *minus ten*.'

He had told himself he wouldn't push it. That he'd leave the whole marriage thing off the table tonight, but his mouth ran away with him.

'My offer still stands. Marry me.'

Grace looked as if she was going to put her head face down in her noodles and cry.

'Not only do I think we can make it work, but I can give you financial security, Grace. You won't have to worry about a house. You could even go back to college or we'd look at investing in a shop, if you wanted. I always liked the idea of opening a shop myself. Of course I always thought it would be a book shop but, hey, I can be flexible. I like cake as much as the next guy.'

She bit her lip.

'And Daisy's college fees would be taken care of. No worries.'

'Noah, I can't—'

'I know it sounds like I'm trying to buy you, but I'm not. Honestly. I need things from you too.'

Her eyes narrowed. 'Such as?'

'Well, there's all the travelling all over the world, staying at nice hotels—Paris, Rome, Sydney—'

Grace sat up straighter. 'Sydney? Do you ever get to visit San Francisco?'

'We could, if you wanted. The other part of the deal is promising to protect me from the scary women with autograph books. Scary women in general, really.'

That was supposed to be a joke. She was supposed to laugh.

'And, of course, there's the all-important bonus…'

She folded her arms. 'Which is?'

He grinned at her. 'Nice teeth,' he said, holding the pose. 'Don't forget the teeth.'

Despite herself, Grace let out a little laugh. 'You're as crazy as a box of frogs.'

'I know,' he said, suddenly sobering. 'This does seem mad—or at least it would if it didn't seem like the sanest idea I've had in a long time.'

Grace's thumbnail made its way to her mouth. The weird thing was he was right. It did sound sane, logical even. Noah was offering her everything she'd ever dreamed of. And she didn't feel guilty about wanting to take it. The situation she was in now wasn't down to lack of hard work, it was merely fate pulling the rug out from under her feet. And, while she would never want to be accused of marrying for money, she had to admit that not having to struggle any more, to be able to enjoy the finer things in life was a real pull.

Oh, what was she going to do?

Noah pushed his plate away. 'If you'd said yes to my original proposal, I'd have expected a longer engagement, time to get used to each other, but if you need somewhere to stay, you can move in with me. Of if you don't like the idea of living together, we'll get married sooner. Whatever works for you, Grace. Just let me know.'

He was being so sweet. And she was on the verge of agreeing with him. She liked Noah. Really liked him. She could maybe even love him—in a growing-old-and-wrinkly-together kind of way. Was that going to be enough?

She'd been paying lip service to the idea of growing up, moving on. Now was her chance to make a mature decision about the rest of her life. Was she going to run away like a frightened child, or was she going to reach out and seize the day?

She exhaled long and hard and looked Noah in the eye.

'I need to talk to Daisy. It wouldn't be fair to make a decision without at least asking her how she feels about the changes this is going to make to her life.'

With a heart rate of at least a hundred and seventy five, Grace dialled Daisy's mobile number. They'd mainly stuck to emails while she'd been away because of the cost of the calls, but this was one thing that couldn't be typed out and sent with the click of a button.

Her stomach went cold and crampy when the dialling tone disappeared and she heard it ringing. A few seconds later a surprisingly crackle-free voice said, 'Mum?'

All at once, Grace began to cry. She missed her girl so much. If only Daisy were here and they could sit round the kitchen table with a pot of tea and a stack of bacon sandwiches and they could hammer this all out.

'Mum! What's happened?'

Grace swallowed the lump in her throat and wiped the tears away with a flat palm. 'Nothing's happened. Well, not nothing—but I mean it's not an emergency—nobody died or anything. I'm just so happy to hear your voice.'

'Oh, Mum, me too!'

And then they were both in tears.

Grace pulled herself together first. There was more purpose to this call than just making her phone wet.

'I've got some news…some good news, I think.'

Daisy sniffed and her voice was sunny through the tears. 'Oh, yes?'

Grace nodded. Stupid, because Daisy couldn't see her. 'You know that man you set me up with…on the blind-date?'

'I thought you weren't dating him.'

'I'm not…well, not really…but we've become very close.' She took a deep breath and the words tumbled out when she released it. 'He's asked me to marry him.'

If Grace thought her heart rate was bad before, it was fit to leap out of her chest now. Not so much the high jump, but hurdling.

'Daisy? Are you still there?'

Silence.

'I'm still here. Flipping hell, Mum. You work fast!'

'It's a long story…'

And Grace filled Daisy in on all the details of The Coffee Bean, who Noah was and how quickly things were likely to happen. When, at last, she'd run out of things to say, she waited.

'I don't care who he is or what he does for a living. Although I have to say I've read a couple of his books and they're really rather good…Anyway, that's beside the point. What really matters is: do you love him?'

Grace dragged her top teeth across her bottom lip. *Not yet, but almost…*

'Not the same way I loved your dad, but I'm older now. I'm looking for something different this time around.'

'And you think you can be happy with him?'

Grace stood still and shut her eyes, trying to picture a future—a long one—with Noah in it.

'Yes. Yes, I think I can.'

She could almost imagine the determined expression on Daisy's face as she said, 'Then I think you should go for it.'

Noah had insisted he pay for Daisy to fly home from Greece for a week and then fly back out again to join her friends. In the days before the wedding they sorted through the flat, packing some things, donating other things to charity shops, just falling about laughing at some of their possessions.

Whose idea had it been to buy the light-up Santa that whistled a tune and dropped his trousers to display a bare bottom when you pushed a button? Grace swore it hadn't been hers. As did Daisy.

It was nice to be back into their old home together, laughing, eating stacks of bacon sandwiches as they worked, but sad too. This truly was goodbye to her old life, the old Grace. Still, she packed a couple of pairs of fishnets, just in case.

Daisy looked up from the box she was packing. 'Mum?'

'Yes, sweetheart?'

'I've also got some news.'

She grabbed her daughter by the shoulders. 'Dear Lord, Daisy! Please tell me you're not getting married or are pregnant!'

Daisy did an eye-roll thing that was totally her. 'Mu-um! Don't be so melodramatic! It's nothing like that. It's big…but it's not bad—at least I don't think it is.'

Grace's heart was pumping. 'Well, get on with it before your poor mother has a heart attack!'

Daisy looked at the floor. 'Being away from home has given me time to think about what I want from life. I've decided I don't want to study history at Durham uni any more.'

'But you're going to do it in London somewhere? That's what you're saying. That's what you're telling me, isn't it?'

She shook her head. 'Sorry, Mum. It's just…not my passion, you know.' She looked up, very earnest, and Grace was reminded of a seven-year-old Daisy who had announced, very seriously, that she would run away if she was made to go to any more of the ballet lessons that Grandma had booked and paid for.

Grace's voice came out soft. 'Then…what is your passion?'

Please don't let her say pole-dancing. Please don't let it be that.

'I missed the café, Mum. I missed the cooking and the smells. I know it's gone now, but I realised I want to learn to cook like you do—to make things, beautiful things that make people happy, even if only for a few minutes.' She looked hopefully at Grace. 'I want to go to catering college like you did.'

Grace's face crumpled into a watery smile. 'Come here, you daft girl!'

Daisy ran into her arms and hugged tight. Grace had resisted the urge to sniff her head, as she'd done when Daisy had been a baby, but now she allowed herself the luxury.

'If that's what you want to do, then it's fine by me. Honest! And if I end up going back to college too, we could end up studying together!'

Daisy stepped back and cocked her head to one side.

'Okay, okay. I get it. You don't want Mum cramping your style at college…But think! One day we could open our own little patisserie together. If you want that, that is.'

Daisy grinned. 'I was hoping you'd say that!'

Grace grinned back at her. 'It's a plan.'

This was wonderful. Perhaps Noah's plan for the future was going to turn out even better than expected. For the first time in weeks, Grace felt hope surge within her.

Grace finished packing her belongings from the flat the night before the wedding. The last thing to go into the last box was the photo of Rob and Daisy that sat in the hallway, keeping guard all these years. Daisy walked up to her mother and hugged her from behind.

Grace's eyes stung. She couldn't quite bring herself to put the frame into the box, so she and Daisy just stared at it for a few wordless minutes.

'It's okay,' Daisy whispered into Grace's ear. 'Dad would have wanted this for you.'

Grace looked down at the photo, at Rob's smiling eyes. They seem to be looking straight at her, connecting with her soul. There wasn't a hint of anger, jealousy or betrayal in them. She knew Daisy was right. But part of her ached for what she'd had with him, that wonderful mix of friendship and passion, completeness and freedom. It felt as if, by marrying Noah, she was saying goodbye to the hope of that in her future, even if, deep down, she hadn't really believed it was possible.

Daisy took the picture from her and laid it in the box. 'It'll be okay, Mum. I promise you. I see the two of you together, and Noah's right for you.

Besides… I've told him that if he ever hurts you, I met a couple of interesting characters in Sicily who would "deal" with him if I asked them.'

Grace burst out laughing and turned to squeeze her daughter to her. 'I love you, Crazy Daisy. And I'll miss you when you go back to Greece and join your friends.'

'But I'm here now, and everything is perfect.'

'Yes, it is,' Grace said and then she folded the flaps of the last box and taped them into place.

The wedding was an uncomplicated affair. Grace and Noah arranged a civil ceremony in the local town hall before a small group of friends and family. Nobody noticed the colour drain from the bride's face as she joined hands with the groom and prepared to say her vows or, if they did, they just put it down to normal wedding jitters.

No one could have known that, at the exact moment of no return, Grace had a premonition so real, so strong, that it left her feeling cold for hours afterwards.

Noah kissed his bride and didn't spot the hint of wariness in her eyes. But Noah wasn't very good at looking below the surface of other people's emotions. And heaven forbid he ever open the trapdoor to the cellar of his own.

The crowd of well-wishers sighed collectively when the groom announced a surprise honeymoon in Paris and whisked an unusually mute Grace away to the station so they could catch Eurostar. By early evening they were in the centre of Paris, the city of lights. The city of love.

Although there were far more expensive hotels on the north side of the river, in the Louvre and Marais *arrondisements*, Noah told Grace he really liked the atmosphere of St Germain, close to the vibrant Latin quarter and full of cafés where philosophers, politicians and great writers of the last few centuries had come to clash minds and share ideas.

'I can't believe I'm really here,' Grace said as they wandered down the Boulevard St Germain, hand in hand. 'All these quaint little cafés with their wicker chairs and awnings and waiters in long white aprons. It's exactly how I imagined it would be.'

Noah just smiled and ushered her down a cobbled side street, round a couple of corners and then into a rather unique-looking restaurant. 'Everyone has to eat at Le Procope at least once,' he explained as the waiter showed them to a table. 'Even if the guidebooks say it's a tourist trap these days. The food is still spectacular.'

Grace stared around the room, one of many which seem to be arranged over several floors in the tall Parisian house. Old paintings of men in dusty wigs covered the walls and ornate glass display cases held china and champagne flutes, giving the impression they were dining in somebody's best parlour.

The food *was* spectacular, from the marinated leek salad to the famous coq au vin, dished up in its very own miniature copper pot. But, after half of her main course, Grace suddenly lost her appetite.

It wasn't long before Noah put down his cutlery and looked at her. In the month since she'd accepted his proposal, she'd come to see this same expression in his eyes over and over again, as if he could reach into her mind and pluck out her thoughts. It was a little unnerving. Extremely unnerving, considering her current train of thought.

'I know this all happened a lot quicker than either of us anticipated, Grace.'

Oh, heck. He knew. She flushed a deep red.

'Tonight... I know it's traditionally our... wedding night, but if you're not ready, if you want to wait a while, that's no problem. We've got the rest of our lives. There's no rush.'

He was being so sweet that Grace wanted to cry. But she didn't think the ever-so-suave French waiters would be impressed if she dissolved into tears and blew her nose on one of the starched white napkins afterwards.

'Thank you, Noah.'

Her heart swelled and, for the first time in the surreal event that had been her second wedding day, she realised with startling clarity that she really was lucky to have found him.

'The truth is… I just don't know how I feel at the moment. It's all been so…'

He reached over the table and took her hand, stroking the ridge of her knuckles with the pad of his thumb. 'I know. Don't worry. We'll both work out how we feel as we go along.'

It was late by the time they got back to the hotel. Grace got dressed for bed in the bathroom, silently cursing the filmy, strappy white thing that Daisy had egged her into buying. After washing her face and brushing her teeth twice, she put the lid on the toilet seat down and sat on it. Her left leg jiggled all on its own.

Deep breathing. That was it. This was no big deal. It was just—

Who was she kidding? She was terrified, the nerves even worse than her *actual* first time. What was wrong with her? Noah was gorgeous and seriously sexy. Didn't she want to sleep with him?

Hell, *yeah*! her ageing hormones chorused.

But still her left leg jiggled.

She pressed down on it with both hands until it stopped, then stood up. When she emerged into the bedroom, Noah was standing, dressed only in dark pyjama bottoms, staring out of one of the long elegant windows.

He turned slowly and she couldn't help noticing the darkening of his pupils, a little *frisson* of electricity that passed between them. He walked over to her, ran a hand across her cheek, down her neck and along her collarbone. Grace stopped breathing. And then he kissed her, long and slow. A perfect kiss. The kind of kiss that certainly should be a prelude to *something*.

But Grace seemed to be standing outside of herself, watching herself, second-guessing what she should do with her hands, where to touch him.

Noah broke the kiss and rested his forehead against hers.

'I'm sorry,' she whispered.

He shook his head and made a soothing noise.

'Really, I am. It's been a long time since it's been my... you know... first time with someone. I'm being stupid, aren't I? It's no big deal. I should... we should... just do it. You know, like ripping the plaster off—'

Noah said nothing, but pressed a finger to her lips. Grace just stared at him. He was doing that thing again—looking inside her. She wanted to screw her eyes up, but she didn't.

He led her to the bed and pulled her down onto it so she was facing away from him and then spooned in behind her.

'Go to sleep, Grace,' he said and pulled her to him with a strong arm.

'But—'

'Go to sleep, Grace.'

Now it seemed her nerves were for nothing, part of her screamed out in frustration. The other part gave a huge sigh of relief. Even though, in their short engagement, they'd spent plenty of time kissing, touching, it still felt a little artificial, a forced situation. And Noah had been travelling some of that time while Grace had needed to stay behind and help wind things up at The Coffee Bean. They really hadn't had a chance to relax with each other, physically or emotionally.

She did it now, letting the tension seep out of her muscles, enjoying the solid feel of him behind her. And, bless him, tucked in as close together as they were, she could tell he was ready for action, even if she wasn't. She pulled his hand into hers and kissed his knuckles, tears in her eyes.

'Night, Noah,' she said in a croaky whisper.

Grace woke in the morning to find Noah still wrapped around her. She twisted so she could look at him. She'd never seen him sleep before. He looked younger, almost boyish—even with the deep creases at the edges of his eyes and the tiny speckling of grey hairs near his temples.

As if he sensed she was watching him, he shifted then opened his eyes. She smiled.

'What's so funny?' he said and pulled a hand from underneath her to rub his eyelids with his fingertips.

'You always look so in control, so self-contained. I kind of like it when you're all groggy and confused.'

He yawned. 'What's the time?'

She leaned over and looked at her watch on the bedside table. 'Nine.'

'Nine!' He jumped out of bed and ran to the bathroom. 'I never sleep in until nine. Seven at the most. You—' he pointed a finger at Grace before disappearing into the bathroom '—must be a bad influence on me.'

Grace lay back on the bed and stretched. He was being lovely. No guilt trip. No tiny reminders that she had chickened out of their wedding night. She decided to play along. 'I do my best to live up to my reputation. Anyway, what's the hurry?'

His head appeared from around the bathroom door. 'Paris. We've only got three days before we go home and I want to show you everything.'

Grace sat up in bed. 'Everything?'

'Well, lots. I need to come back here in around three months' time for a book launch, so anything we miss now, we can do then.' He looked her up and down. 'What are you waiting for?'

Grace folded her arms across her chest. 'Coffee. I'm not going anywhere until I've had coffee.'

They went out for breakfast and had warm croissants and strong black coffee at Les Deux Magots.

They climbed the Eiffel Tower, marvelled at Monet's waterlilies and ate ham baguettes and cold Belgian beer sitting under bright red canopies in an outdoor café in the Jardin Tuileries.

Noah had done all these things before, but doing them with Grace brought a freshness to the experience. She flung herself headlong into every sight, every sound, every taste. There was one place he was desperate to take her, but he was saving it for last.

Since they were close by, they wandered round the Louvre, even braving the crowds to remark on how much smaller than expected the Mona Lisa was and wondering what the Venus de Milo's arms really would have been doing had they not been lost, and if anyone had actually found them and not realised what they were.

But, even in the face of such a wonderful day, Noah felt a little sad for Grace. She really ought to be here with someone who could give her the romance he feared she secretly craved. But he was selfish. She may have settled for second best with him, but he didn't want to let her go so she could find it with someone else.

By three o'clock, Grace went on sightseeing strike. They were back in the Jardin Tulieries, the vast building of the Louvre behind them, and she sat down on a low backless bench amidst the trees and refused to budge.

He tugged at her hand until she consented to stand up. 'One more stop.'

'Do we have to?' she said, her voice muffled by his jacket as she leaned against him.

'We do. Come on, it's just across the Rue de Rivoli.'

Under the large stone façaded arcades of the Rue de Rivoli was a place that was as close to heaven on earth as Grace could get. Angelina. The café famous for the best hot chocolate in Paris, and the pastries! Oh, the pastries!

It was all Noah could do to get her off the street and in through the door. But she found the inside was just as fabulous, with an ornate curved counter filled with works of art. Pink macaroons, stuffed with raspberries and topped with delicate flecks of silver leaf, pistachio bombes the colour of fresh green shoots with contrasting pink icing, éclairs, mille feuille, tartes…It was almost criminal that anyone should think of eating them.

When they were seated at a small round table beside a square ivory column, Grace had no problem in deciding what she should order. It had to be their signature dish, Mont Blanc, accompanied by Chocolat Chaud des Africains. When it arrived, she spent a good minute memorising every swirl in the chestnut purée covering the fluffy white meringue before daring to break into it with her fork. The hot chocolate was just as good: thick gloopy melted chocolate—none of this powdered nonsense—infused with spices and served in individual jugs accompanied by glasses of whipped cream to dollop into it. She didn't understand the reason for the glass of cold water the waiter served her. But then she tasted the hot chocolate. It had a wonderfully thick bitter taste, but a sip of cool water was definitely needed every now and then to clear her palate.

Noah had been going to order just coffee, complaining he'd eaten enough sweet stuff already in the last few months, but she wouldn't let him off the hook. He smiled at her, and she knew he liked it when she got bossy, so she grinned back at him.

He'd done this for her, had planned it all out. A trip to Angelina was all the wedding present she could have wished for. Just like that, all her fears about the future melted away and the anchors holding her in the past let go. This was her life now. This was her husband. And he was funny and caring and sexy enough to eat with a dollop of whipped cream.

She couldn't stop looking at him as he paid the bill and they made their way through the crowded café to the front of the shop. She didn't even break her stride to look at the cakes behind the counter again. She was totally focused on him.

The cool spring breeze was welcome on her face when they stepped back out into the street. She stopped him by tugging his hand, making him come back to her. Now it was her turn to call the shots, to bestow the gift. She leaned in close and kissed his ear before whispering, 'Take me back to the hotel, Noah.'

'But—'

'Take me back to the hotel.'

All the way back in the taxi, they held hands, played with each other's fingers, unable to stop touching, caressing, stroking. For most of the journey they just smiled and stared out of the window, but they saw nothing, their whole attention given to the tips of their bodies that were intertwined.

It was the same in the lift at the hotel. They stood at the back, behind the other guests, and shared a secret with each other.

Once in the hotel room, there was no place for nerves. Grace didn't even remember she'd had any as they began to kiss and peel layer upon layer of clothing from each other. Sometimes they were hungry and impatient, sometimes slow and teasing.

She was lost. Lost somewhere where there was only Noah. Noah's hands, Noah's lips.

When the last of the barriers between them had been stripped away, he slid his hands down her naked torso and she shivered with delight. Then he scooped her up in his arms so she was cradled against his heartbeat and carried her to the bed.

CHAPTER SEVEN

MAKING love with Noah was like nothing else Grace had ever experienced. It was like handling raw fire, but without getting scorched—well, only in a good way. He was so strong, so totally focused, yet so devastatingly good that, for a few moments, she was incoherent with pleasure. Her whole body thrummed.

She could feel his breath against her shoulder as he lay half-draped over her. His ribs moved up and down, up and down, in a deep, even rhythm. Grace lay still, taking comfort from it, and let her eyes wander over her surroundings. Light from a street lamp somewhere shone on the ceiling and wall, creating a strip of distorted light, and she stared at it, wondering why she'd woken and why she couldn't snuggle back into him and sleep.

With Rob, sex had been good—fun, energetic, playful—but this…Noah…

A different league.

She couldn't kid herself any more. This was no

platonic, mutual partnership. This was the real thing. With honest-to-goodness violins playing and birds singing, even though it was nowhere near dawn yet.

She loved Noah.

And so much for it being safe. It was grown up, all right. Big and scary and very, very dangerous with sharp teeth. No wonder she'd made excuses to avoid getting close to it all these years. She should have listened to her instincts and stayed the hell away.

But then Noah made a sound that was half-snuffle, half-snore and pulled her tighter against him and she couldn't help but smile, even as her eyes filled with tears. Why did the good things in life have to come with a dark opposite? Life and death. Love and hate. Fear and faith. Why couldn't she love Noah without the threat of losing him? It would always be there, hanging in the background like an unexploded bomb, waiting to detonate when she finally relaxed and believed it had all been a bluff.

Losing Rob had been bad enough. For months, she'd only dragged herself out of bed in the mornings because Daisy had needed her cereal. Daisy had saved her life back then without even knowing it. Any moments of imbalance on her mother's part had been quickly countered by a ponytail of dark waves and a cheeky smile.

Grace wriggled herself backwards so she was as close to Noah as she could get, not even a millimetre of air between them. His chest was warm against her back and beating a reassuring rhythm.

Not yet. Not tonight. But the loss would come. One day. It always did.

And she was a coward, too scared to face it.

She gently kissed the forearm wrapped around her and pulled it close so she could lay her cheek against it.

You should have seen it coming, Grace. You do love and marriage and babies, remember? What did you think was going to happen?

Her only hope was that Noah was taking the same journey she was, that they were going to do as he'd said and work out how they felt together.

The next couple of days were exactly what a honeymoon in Paris should be. Grace and Noah stayed in bed and ordered room service quite a lot, making love whenever the mood took them, which seemed to be pretty often. Even Daisy would have been shocked that her old fogey of a mother could have such an appetite for nothing but Noah. Not that she was going to talk to Daisy about this. In Daisy's own words, that would be TMI—too much information. For both of them.

On their last morning, after breakfast in bed, which had turned into *we might as well stay here for lunch too*, Grace snuggled into Noah, her head on his chest and his arm tucked round her.

Even though they were married, there was so much she didn't know about him. It had all happened so quickly that they'd bypassed a lot of the getting-to-know-you process. And she wanted to know everything about him, to understand him. Partly because she was hoping he was feeling the same way she was, but it was more than that. She loved him. And that meant every new thing she learned about him was a treasure, something precious to be stored away in her mind and wondered at.

'You know all about me now—my history with Rob, my disastrous dates between then and now—but you haven't told me anything about you.' She poked him in the ribs. 'That's the problem with being such a nosy parker. You're too good a listener. And I'm too good a talker.'

Noah stroked her arm and kissed the top of her head. 'Seems we've found the perfect balance.'

She shook her head against his chest. 'You must have had a couple of serious relationships in your life. I can't be the first one. And, anyway, I don't really count yet, do I?'

A pair of hands reached round her waist and hoisted her up so she was lying on top of him. A wicked gleam was in his eye. 'Believe me, you count.' And then he started to trail his fingers up the backs of her legs, higher, higher…

'That's not what I meant, Noah. You're avoiding the issue.'

His fingers stopped moving. 'Maybe there's nothing to avoid.'

But the gleam in his eye had been replaced by a shuttered hardness. She slid off him. 'Maybe there is,' she said quietly.

Noah pushed himself on to one elbow and launched himself out of bed. 'I don't want to talk about it, Grace. Subject closed.'

She gathered the rumpled sheet around her as he disappeared into the bathroom and slammed the door. Well, there was her answer. Now she knew exactly how Noah felt.

The face staring back at him from the bathroom mirror was not a pretty sight. His brows were slanted together and his jaw was square and hard.

It had started already.

The probing. The questions.

He just hadn't thought it would happen so soon. Grace had taken him completely by surprise. They'd been having such a good time, just enjoying the moment, and she'd had to go and spoil it with deep and meaningful stuff. Although he knew he shouldn't be—she was just doing what women did—he was angry with her.

It had taken Sara much longer to start trying to unravel him but, after a while, the innocent-sounding enquiries had come. What are you thinking, Noah? What are you *feeling*, Noah? It was like being one giant scab that women couldn't resist picking at.

At first, he'd tried really hard with Sara. He'd tried to dig deep, had tried to come up with answers she'd like. But it hadn't been real. He'd invented a version of himself—fictional Noah—whom he'd analysed like one of the characters he created in his books. The real Noah was just as much a mystery to himself as he was to Sara.

So he'd thought hard about fictional Noah's motivation and what he wanted out of life. He'd prepared pretty speeches to say in case she caught him unawares. Things that Sara wanted to hear, things that would make her happy. After a while he'd got fed up with fictional Noah. The guy had been just too annoyingly perfect.

Maybe that was why his smokescreen had failed after a couple of years. He'd just got sick of the sound of his own voice and he couldn't stand to regurgitate all that soppy stuff any longer. Then Sara had started talking about glass walls and needing more. She'd picked and picked and picked at him. And when she'd finished gouging away at him, when the scab had finally lifted, she'd discovered the truth. Underneath, there was nothing. And then she'd left.

He really didn't want Grace to leave.

The last couple of days had been amazing and, despite his glass wall, he'd felt closer to the love thing than he'd ever felt before. But still there was something stopping him. He just wasn't that deep. There was nothing there to give.

So, he'd just have to distract her or, like Sara, she'd pick, pick, pick and discover what was under the scab that had reformed itself into a hard little shell. No healthy new skin. Just an empty space.

He took a shower to give himself and Grace a few minutes to calm down. As he towel-dried himself he hoped to God she wasn't crying. Anything he said to crying women just sounded trite. He normally made things worse.

But Grace wasn't crying when he re-entered the bedroom. She was getting dressed—noisily. She was banging doors and stomping from wardrobe to bed and back. He intercepted her.

'I'm sorry, Grace. I didn't mean to snap at you.'

See? Even though the words weren't over-the-top and gushy, they still sounded fake to his ears, like lines in a play. It wasn't that he didn't mean them, just…that he didn't feel anything when he said them.

She stopped and looked at him, a shoe in one hand. He suddenly felt as if he'd been sliced up, put on a slide and shoved under a microscope.

'I appreciate the apology. I wasn't trying to pry. I just think we need to get to know each other better.'

He nodded.

He'd thought he'd be safe from that with Grace. Safe, because a marriage based on nothing to do with love shouldn't require all the painful scab-picking. He'd been wrong. The thought niggled him. He didn't like being wrong on a general level, but also about this specific thing. If he'd got this wrong, what else was he mistaken about?

Time to distract.

'Let's go for a walk,' he said.

They ended up wandering up to the Seine and onto Les Pont Des Arts. Grace leaned on the railing and watched the slate-grey water rushing below the bridge. Then she raised her head and looked towards the Ille de la Cite, the spires of Notre Dame and Sainte-Chapelle poking into the sky. It was so beautiful here, all this pale grey stone, the deep blue of the sky, the vibrant green of the trees that lined the river.

Noah came up beside her and they stared at the water in silence.

He seemed so relaxed, so charming. And she'd not seen anything beneath that until today. It was like the river. She'd been too blinded by the ripples and light bouncing off the surface to see what nasty stuff was lurking at the bottom. There were huge parts of himself that Noah kept hidden and she wanted to know why. She wanted to know why he camouflaged himself so well.

Noah reached out and took her hand.

She didn't pull away, even though she was still smarting from his remark that morning. She accepted his hand, curling her fingers around his warm skin. He was trying, and that was good enough for now.

They walked to the end of the bridge and down a flight of stone steps so they were walking on the grey stone quay right next to the Seine. Other couples passed them, hands caught just like theirs, and Grace knew she should feel a sense of comradeship with them.

I'm in Paris and in love too.

But it wasn't quite the same, was it? Those other couples were in love with each other.

Now they were close to the silver birches lining the bank she could see that their markings were not just the normal black slits in the pearly bark. Up the entire trunks of every tree, covering every possible square inch, were names and declarations of love in many different languages and scripts. She recognised some English and French and Japanese, but others she just couldn't put a name to. She'd bet Noah would know. But Noah wasn't looking at the trees; he was looking at the river and muttering something about Napoleonic architecture.

An echo of the premonition from her wedding day turned her toes to ice.

Noah didn't love her.

He might never love her.

And he would never carve her name on a tree in Paris.

Back in London, things improved—at least on the surface. Noah and Grace began their lives together. They ate at nice restaurants, attended parties and other functions up in town, and generally stuck to the plan they'd had when they'd married. Noah wrote and Grace started looking at prospectuses for catering colleges, even though she wasn't sure any more that she wanted to go back to being a student, but it seemed she should explore the option, even if she didn't pursue it.

And they made love.

For Grace, it was the only thing that kept the creeping cold feeling at bay. Unfortunately, it wasn't helping with the head-over-heels, desperately in love with Noah thing. It was all such a cliché. Every time he looked at her now, her heart did a triple flip. When he smiled, she just wanted to melt. And when he took her in his arms and touched her with such tenderness, she thought her heart would break with the beauty of it.

In other words, she was up the creek without a paddle. And she was just crazy enough in love with him to want to jump out of the boat and drown in him. She just didn't care.

But they never spoke of love. It was an unwritten rule. Not part of their agreement.

One morning, almost a month after their return from Paris, Grace decided there was only so much mooching around a big old house that a woman could do. Noah was hidden away inside his study, as he often was in the mornings, wrestling with some character problem that was making him a huge grouch, and she knocked on the door and let him know she was going into town. He just waved with his left hand and continued scribbling in a notebook with his right. She didn't take offence. She was starting to get used to the Noah who retreated into his imaginary world for hours every day.

Walking up the cobbles in the High Street made her sad now. The Coffee Bean and Martin's book shop, which had also been snapped up, were now boarded up. It wouldn't be long before the Java Express logos appeared on them. It felt as if a part of the village's soul had died.

Without warning, tears filled Grace's eyes and she began to sob.

What was happening to her? Yes, she was an emotional kind of person, but she wasn't normally given to weeping in the street. Maybe it was all getting too much for her—the pain of seeing Noah, blithely going about his business, never realising for a second that she wasn't totally happy, despite his best efforts to give her all the things he'd promised her. She wouldn't want to be without him. She loved him too much to leave him and still held out hope that, given a few years, he would soften and come to love her too. But she was starting to think that her grown-up decision to marry Noah for companionship and security hadn't been her most sensible moment. After all, even grown-ups made mistakes.

A yawn crept up on her. She was tired, that was all. And, she had to face it, there was plenty in her life at the moment that was contributing to her general weariness. It was probably just PMT making her all emotional. She'd been through a major upheaval in the last couple of months—losing her job, moving house, getting married. No wonder she was wiped out and falling into bed before ten in the evening.

Grace walked down the High Street in the clear fresh sunshine that only came with a gentle English summer's day. It was too nice to spend the morning cooped up in little boutiques, looking for ever more cocktail dresses to wear to Noah's writing bashes, so she kept walking and made for the common. The wind was blowing the long grass flat, first this direction and then that. She chose one of the paths of short grass that had probably marked the common for hundreds of years and followed it.

The school holidays were still a couple of weeks away and it was relatively quiet, with only the playground a source of noise. She chose a bench on the far side of the common, with a view of the pretty little church, far enough away from both the Tiger's Head pub and the playground to be quiet and to have very little traffic. The sun was just peeping over the tops of the houses, sending vanilla rays to warm everything, and she just sat back and closed her eyes, drinking it in.

Despite the practically idyllic surroundings, tears gathered beneath her lids and pushed their way between her lashes to trickle down her cheeks. She smudged them away with her palms. Damn this PMT. It wasn't helping things at all, it really wasn't.

Since relaxing seemed to be beyond her, she decided to look in her diary and check when this hormone-induced dementia was likely to be relieved. She pulled the little book out of her handbag on the seat beside her and flicked through the pages until she found the current week. Then she went back a week and stared at that page. No, that couldn't be right. And then she flipped back another week.

According to her diary, she was—she counted the days with her finger, flipping over onto the current page—thirteen days late.

Late. And not one or two days—thirteen!

Still, she'd never been like clockwork. It was probably just stress. There'd been times when she'd been so stressed that her cycle had gone completely out of whack. However, in recent years, she'd never had a reason to worry that it had been anything *but* stress.

Stop being so overdramatic! There weren't any other symptoms—such as the overwhelming urge for anything starchy like she'd had when she'd been expecting Daisy. This was just panic talking. Any time now, her period would start and she'd laugh at herself for even considering that…

She flipped back to the pages to when she'd been in Paris. Okay, so that would have been slap-bang in the middle of her cycle, but it didn't mean anything. They'd been careful. Okay, considering she'd been very *careless* with her heart, careful probably wasn't a good word to use in connection with Noah, but they'd used protection. She was just worrying over nothing.

Grace put the diary back in her bag and stood up. There was a late-opening chemist three doors down from The Coffee Bean. No, where The Coffee Bean had once been. She'd just pop in. Not that she really needed to. It was just that, with everything else in her life at the moment, she really didn't need one more thing to keep her tossing and turning at night.

Grace sneaked into the kitchen late that night, Daisy's laptop under her arm. Noah had dozed off in front of a war film on telly. She logged onto Blinddatebrides.com and sent up a prayer that, even though it wasn't their usual day to chat, Dani and Marissa would be online.

Blinddatebrides.com is running 12 chat rooms, 26 private IM conferences, and 5216 members are online.

Grace looked at the little header she normally glossed over and laughed out loud. Blinddatebrides.com, indeed! Not only had she found a groom, but she'd come away from one of their set-ups with a little more than she'd bargained for.

She sent an email SOS out to the girls and waited.

Englishcrumpet invites Kangagirl and Sanfrandani to a private IM conference.
Englishcrumpet: Anybody out there?

Grace inhaled, breathed out and waited. By the time she was just starting to run out of oxygen, there was a ping from the laptop.

Kangagirl: What's the emergency? Grace?
Englishcrumpet: We'd better wait and see if Dani shows up. I'm not sure I can do this twice.
Kangagirl: Now you're scaring me.
Englishcrumpet: I'm a little freaked out myself.

A second ping announced Dani's arrival.

Sanfrandani: Hi, guys!
Kangagirl: Grace is just about to drop a bombshell. She's gone all mysterious and dramatic.
Sanfrandani: Bigger than the I'm-getting-married-to-Noah bombshell?
Englishcrumpet: Way bigger. But kind of related.
Kangagirl: Don't leave us in suspense, Grace!

Grace looked down at her stomach. There was another thing that would be getting bigger shortly. Here goes, she thought.

Englishcrumpet: I'm pregnant.

Once again, she'd stunned them into silence. If there were awards for that kind of thing, Grace was sure she'd get a medal.

Englishcrumpet: Say something!
Sanfrandani: Congratulations?
Kangagirl: How? I mean...oh, you know what I mean.
Englishcrumpet: Kinda relieved you're not asking for a blow-by-blow account there, Marissa!
Sanfrandani: You're not taking this well, are

*you? The more flippant you get, the worse
things are, usually.*

Grace stared at the home pregnancy test she'd
propped up by the laptop screen, just to make sure she
hadn't been seeing things. Tests had moved on quite
a lot since she'd last taken one and now they were
practically idiot-proof, no faint little blue or pink
lines to count, just a big digital screen reading:
PREGNANT. It might as well have added, *You,
Dummy!* The pregnancy tests might be idiot-proof,
but the people who needed them obviously weren't.
Why else would a forty-year-old woman have got
herself into a situation better suited to a reckless
teenager?

*Englishcrumpet: I'm trying to get my head
round it, to be honest. Humour seems to be the
only way to stop myself losing the plot entirely.*
Sanfrandani: Have you told Noah?
*Englishcrumpet: I haven't told anyone! Not
even Daisy! What if she doesn't want a little
brother or sister stealing her limelight?*
*Kangagirl: If Daisy is half the girl you've
brought her up to be, she'll be wonderful!*
Sanfrandani: And Noah?
*Englishcrumpet: Dani, do you have to be the
voice of reason* all *the time?*

*Englishcrumpet: Sorry, that was meant to be
a joke, but it just came across snippy.
Sanfrandani: No offence taken. I can tell
you're scared witless.
Kangagirl: You can't not tell your husband,
Grace. He's going to notice eventually.*

Grace sagged. She had no idea if Noah had ever
had any thoughts about becoming a parent. They'd
both just assumed it wouldn't be part of the
package. And that had been fine with her, but now—
even though Dani was right, she was scared
witless—part of her was desperate to make it part
of the package and hope that Noah would agree.
Maybe a baby would help. He couldn't help but
break out of his cold, tight little shell with a son or
a daughter to love.

*Englishcrumpet: I'm not sure how he's going
to feel about this.
Sanfrandani: Don't be too hard on him if he's
a little shocked. After all, you're feeling the
same way yourself. But think, what a wonderful way to start your new life together!
Kangagirl: Oh, Grace! I'm so happy for you!
The man of your dreams and a new little baby
on the way.*

God bless Marissa and Dani. Perhaps they were
right. Perhaps her dreams could come true.

But then reality slapped her round the face and made her sit up.

Dreams. She'd just got used to thinking about having some of those. A new career. Time to herself. They were just going to have to go on hold for another eighteen years or so. If she wasn't so confused about how to tell Noah, about what to tell Noah, she'd be in fits of laughter. Oh, the irony of it—the empty-nester who'd finally gathered up the courage to find her wings suddenly had another chick to hatch.

Noah woke the next morning to find Grace stroking his thigh, a naughty little smile on her face. He grinned back at her. This was better. In recent weeks Grace had been less and less like herself, and the last few days she'd been positively testy. Whatever had been bothering her was obviously dealt with.

He didn't mind forgoing his morning run for a little bit of exercise with Grace, not one little bit.

Afterwards, when they were wrapped round each other and he was starting to doze, she lifted her head from his chest and looked at him.

'Are you happy, Noah?'

He nodded. Yes, he was. Not just in the afterglow of great sex, but with his life generally. There'd been a few hiccups at the beginning of their marriage—

teething problems, he supposed—but now it looked as if things were back on track.

She sat up a little so she could focus on his face properly and he rolled over a little to face her. She licked her lower lip and then stuck her thumbnail in her mouth. After nibbling it for a few seconds, a tiny frown deepening between her eyebrows, she pulled it out again.

'I have some news,' she finally said.

His eyebrows raised. 'Good news or bad news?'

'Um…Depends very much on how you feel about it.'

'Well, why don't you tell me what it is and I will tell you how I feel about it?' he said in a voice as smooth as clotted cream.

'You'll tell me how you really feel?'

'Yes.' Or at least he'd tell her what he thought. That would just have to do.

She took a deep breath. 'I'm pregnant.'

The world seemed to freeze for a second and, when it got going again, he was sure it was revolving in the wrong direction.

'I'm sorry?'

Grace pulled the sheet up over her chest and held it with clenched fists. 'We're going to have a baby. I'm pregnant.'

A baby? How was that…? When had they…?

'But…how could you be? We used—'

Grace lost her forlorn expression and became a

bit more like the sassy woman he'd gone on a blind date with. 'Only ninety-eight per cent effective. It says so on the box.'

'But…'

'You said you were going to tell me how you feel.'

He blinked. Something instinctive rushed through Noah. Something primal, fierce and protective. But he didn't know what to call it. And it terrified the life out of him. She didn't really want to know that, did she? That he was feeling strange things—especially fear. That wouldn't help at all.

And that wasn't actually what she'd been asking. She'd be cross with him if he was brutally honest. Just like Sara always had been. Damn these women and their subtexts.

He got out of bed and put on his robe, tying the knot just a little too tightly for comfort. So he retied it, looser this time. He needed to process this, to understand this strange tug inside him. Anchoring it in something real, in facts and figures, might help.

'Do you know when we got…erm…?'

'Pregnant is the word you're looking for, Noah.'

Grace gathered the sheet around her and stood up too. That was the first time she'd done that. She'd never bothered hiding her body from him before, not even right at the beginning.

'Paris, I think. What difference does it make?'

Somehow it helped to know, to analyse. To work

out where the turning point had been, the moment at which everything had changed, even if he hadn't realised it at the time. It was the way he looked at his characters, understood what was happening to them. Perhaps it would help him to understand what he was feeling, this new thing that made his eyes prickle and his heart pump. Was he going to cry? He never cried.

A look of exquisite pain passed across Grace's features.

'Come here,' he said, opening his arms.

Grace looked wary but she shuffled over to him, the sheet tangling in her feet, and let him hold her. He could feel her breath moist against his chest.

'Don't worry.' He smoothed her hair with the flat of his hand, long strokes that travelled down her shoulders and onto her back. 'We can deal with this. We'll work through this.'

And then he laid a kiss on the top of her head and stepped back.

'I need to…I think I'll…I'm going for a run.'

We'll work through this?

Grace stared at the bedroom door with her mouth open. He'd made it sound as if this was a problem with their taxes or a lost passport. She'd told him they were going to have a baby and he'd gone for a run? Unbelievable!

She sat down on the edge of the bed and folded the sheet around her.

What a difference from when she'd told Rob they were expecting Daisy. It had been only days before their first wedding anniversary, and Rob had whooped with joy when she'd told him. He'd picked her up and swung her round, only to stop and place her on the sofa as if she were delicate porcelain. He'd apologised a dozen times and kissed her twenty more before phoning everyone he knew to brag.

Grace twisted the sheet between her fists. What was it with her new husband? What was he afraid of? That she'd have less time for him? Was he jealous? She just didn't get it.

Her hands wandered to her stomach. Not exactly flat, but as flat as a woman her age was likely to have. Almost twenty years would separate her two children, but she was as connected now to the tiny life inside her that was only a bundle of promise as she was to the one outside her who was fulfilling that promise by exploring her potential. And it was an even greater joy finding out this time, because she knew all the wonderful times waiting for her in the future.

This was her baby.

Well, at least Noah's reaction had an upside.

Now she knew how she felt about being pregnant. She wanted this baby more than anything. She wanted to feel its kick, to feel it moving inside her. She wanted to hear its first cry and feel that total rush of love when they first met.

She stood up and went in search of underwear. Noah would show his excitement sooner or later, wouldn't he? Perhaps Dani was right and he was just poleaxed by her announcement. Whatever the problem was, she hoped he would be in a better state of mind when he came back from his run.

Noah's feet pounded on the hard paving slabs. He glanced up the road, saw there was a gap in the traffic and sprinted across and onto the cricket pitch. Grace was pregnant. With a baby. His baby. He wasn't sure if he wanted to jump up a tree and do a Tarzan yell or go and buy cigars.

At least you're feeling something.

Shut up.

But this changed everything. What about the trips all over the world? The parties and awards ceremonies? He hadn't ever envisioned doing that with a pushchair in one hand and a nappy bag over his shoulder.

You're being selfish.

I know. Shut up.

He ran faster, harder, until the breath sliced cold in his lungs and his thigh muscles burned. He'd never considered becoming a father. Although his own had been a poor example, at least the comparison with friends' dads had given him an idea of what a father *should* be. He should be able to interact with his son, praise him, talk to him, teach him about life. Not freeze him out and act as if he didn't exist most of the time, even when the boy did his very best to make him proud.

Noah stopped running and rested his hands on his thighs, panting. But the feeling that he was pounding, churning, moving stayed with him. It was as if darkness were coming up from the inside of him, threatening to overtake him. He didn't like it. He didn't like it at all. This feeling was darker than the one he'd felt when Grace had told him she was expecting his child. Whatever this feeling was, he'd better outrun it.

Fear. What you're feeling is fear.

Well, he had good reason to be afraid. When that baby was born and Grace expected him to be all those things a father should be, she was going to find out. He wouldn't be able to disguise the emptiness any longer. She'd know. And then she wouldn't want him any more. Neither of them would.

And, with that thought ringing in his ears, Noah started sprinting again, even though he hadn't really caught his breath.

Blinddatebrides.com is running 16 chat rooms, 28 private IM conferences, and 6217 members are online.

Sanfrandani: So what happened after he got back from his run?
Englishcrumpet: He apologised and he was really lovely to me. He took me into town and bought me lunch. This morning he appeared with a little toy bunny for the baby's cot.
Kangagirl: Awwww! It sounds as if he's really coming round to the idea.

It did, didn't it? Then why didn't it *feel* right? Why were her alarm bells clanging? Why had the cold spread from her toes up to her knees?

Englishcrumpet: I know. But it's not that simple. You didn't see his face when I told him.
Sanfrandani: He was bound to be surprised. You were.
Englishcrumpet: How can I explain this? It's like there's…a wall. Between him and me. He's doing all the right things, saying all the right things, but it feels as if he's just going through the motions. As if he's…I don't know…papering over the cracks.
Kangagirl: Give him time, Grace! He sounds like he's doing his best.

Oh, flip! Tears were dropping on the keyboard of the laptop. Daisy would kill her if she fritzed this thing.

Kangagirl: Grace, if anyone can melt his heart back, it's you.

Sanfrandani: And you know we're here for you night and day, whenever you need to talk.

Englishcrumpet: Thanks, girls! You've got me in tears here!

Sanfrandani: Snap!

Kangagirl: Me too!!!!!!

Englishcrumpet: One day I'm going to meet up with you two and give you the biggest hug ever. You'll have to peel me off and restrain me before I crush you to death like a python.

Kangagirl: Sounds fab!

Sanfrandani: It's a date!

Grace logged off and wiped her eyes. She would just have to give Noah some room. She knew without a doubt that if she pushed him to open up he would just push back harder. So she'd wait. They had over seven months until the baby came. Surely they'd make some progress by then.

CHAPTER EIGHT

OVER the next few weeks a truce developed. Grace stayed on the fringes, gave Noah room. Noah took the room she offered, but it never seemed that he came any closer to making a step in her direction. Not really.

The hormones really started to kick in, though. Her pregnancy with Daisy had been a bit of a breeze, but her body was older and crabbier now and it protested loudly at being stretched and changed and fed upon by an invader. Noah tried hard, but he was struggling to keep up with the mood swings, his new wife one minute sweet and affectionate, the next snarling and crying. The waists of some of her trousers and skirts were already tight and she'd woken up one morning to discover she'd gone up a cup size—one change that hadn't flummoxed Noah, quite the opposite, actually.

It was just as well she didn't have to go to work, because even getting out of bed before ten made her want to heave. It got better in the afternoons, but she was suddenly so picky about her food. One minute she wanted something with a ravenous craving, the next thing she'd go green at the sight of it.

She crawled down to the kitchen one morning and slumped on the big oak table Noah had told her they'd had to hoist in through the windows when he'd bought it. It wasn't long before Noah appeared from his study, looking disgustingly well-groomed, even if he did have the largest scowl she'd ever seen on his face. He came over and kissed her on the cheek, anyway. She knew it wasn't personal, that his head was trapped somewhere between his book and the real world.

'Problems?' she said, yawning in the middle of the word.

Noah nodded. 'It's my maddening hero. He just won't behave.'

Grace lay her forehead on the table. Know how that feels, she thought. 'What's he up to now?'

Noah sat down at the table. 'Are you feeling okay? Do you want me to get you something?'

She shook her head very slightly and it squeaked on the surface of the table. 'No. Tell me about Karl the rebellious hero. It'll help to have something to distract me. Why can't you get him to work?'

'It's the love sub-plot. You know…where he gets involved with the woman who's a double agent. It's just not convincing. *He's* not convincing.'

Grace sat up slowly. 'Can you take that bit out?'

'No.' Noah shook his head. 'The betrayal aspect, when she turns him over to his enemies, is important to the central plot.'

'I'm no expert at spy novels, Noah. But perhaps you need a woman's perspective.'

He looked so boyishly hopeful she would have run round the table and kissed him if she'd been able to move that fast without throwing up.

'Would you?'

'Of course. I'm no good to anyone at the moment. I might as well curl up on the sofa and read a good book.' And get to see how your mind works before the manuscript has been meticulously polished and made presentable, she silently added.

He jumped up, kissed her cheek and then rushed out of the room. 'I'll print it off!' he yelled from somewhere down the corridor.

Grace spent the most wonderful day in the high-ceilinged drawing room, lying on the sofa with a throw over her. It was blissfully sunny outside and Noah opened the French windows for her so the warm air blew in the scent of flowers from the garden. She read his whole manuscript—well, apart from a bit in chapter twenty, where it stopped mid-sentence in the middle of a fight scene and then carried on a few days later. Apparently Noah needed to do some more research on a certain gadget before he could write the rest of that.

Noah had been pacing in the doorway too much

so she'd shooed him away, sent him in to town to get some food for dinner. She'd discovered he was a much better cook than she'd imagined, but that was hardly surprising. He liked to use all the wonderful fresh organic ingredients. She'd hardly been able to get creative with the food on her budget over the years. There was a limit to the amount of things you could do with baked beans.

By the time Noah returned home with bags of groceries, Grace was sitting in the kitchen sipping tea, feeling considerably perkier.

'What did you think?' he said, looking a little nervous.

'What did you buy?' she replied with a mischevious wink. 'I'm famished.'

'Oh, it's like that, is it?'

'Yes, it is. You tell me what you're cooking me for tea and I'll tell you what I think of Karl the spy.'

'Minx,' he muttered as he opened the fridge and started shoving vegetables inside. But he dived into a carrier bag and produced a whole chicken. 'Yesterday night, you were waxing lyrical about old-fashioned roast dinners…'

Grace screwed her face up and made a gagging noise, which turned out to be a really bad idea, because thinking about the pink, dimpled, slightly cold, slightly pink chicken in its packaging was making her feel queasy.

'Thought so,' Noah said and shoved it back in the

bag, out of view. 'That's why I got this…' And, with a flourish, he pulled a bag of fresh pasta and a handful of ripe tomatoes out of a different bag.

Grace jumped up. 'I love you!'

Noah stuttered.

'I mean…I love what you chose for dinner.' She shrugged, the fake smile on her face making her feel just as iffy as the chicken had. What a stupid thing to say. And the look on his face—pure horror—as if she'd jumped up and said, *I want to cut your left leg off!*

She had to pull things back, pretend she hadn't said it and that everything was normal between them. Although normal for them wasn't quite like any other marriage she knew. She made her voice light and breezy.

'It was just what I wanted. How did you know?'

His face relaxed slightly and she breathed out. 'I don't know. I just did.'

'How about you start chopping and I'll tell you my thoughts on your book over dinner?'

'Oh, no. That wasn't the deal.'

'Well, I'm so hungry I'm feeling a little nauseous so, if you want to do this now, you may have to break off to hold my hair back—'

'Okay! It's a deal. That's all I need to know.'

Noah watched as Grace twirled linguine onto her fork.

'I think I know what your hero's problem is.'

'You do?'

She popped the pasta in her mouth and chewed. When she'd swallowed, she said, 'He's too concerned with protecting himself, staying close to what he knows. He's been trained to deal with the situation he faces with the girl, hasn't he? And he always stays within the boundaries of that training, within his comfort zone.'

Noah put down his fork and stared at her. 'But if I make him forget his training, he's bad at his job and that makes him unsympathetic as a hero.'

She shook her head and put her own cutlery down so she could wave her hands. 'I'm not saying he should be bad at his job. I'm saying that he needs to have a good reason to *ignore* his training, make himself vulnerable. You need to dig deeper.'

Noah snorted. 'You sound like my editor.'

'You know I'm right.'

Yeah, yeah. He did. His inner Rottweiler was in a frenzy, trying to get him to listen. Dig deeper. He'd been living with this character for months now. He wasn't sure there was any 'deeper' to go. What did he do if Karl the spy turned out to be just like his creator?

Well, just like him, Karl would be stuffed.

Noah was being ratty with Martine and he knew it. She also knew it, and had no problems letting him know she knew. He snapped at her while she went through the diary for the next couple of weeks with him and reminded him of the details of his speaking engagement that evening in Manchester.

But Noah was too busy playing with Post-it notes stuck to a whiteboard on his office wall. Laying his story out visually on coloured squares of paper helped him get a feel for its shape, its rhythm. He was flexing his mental shovel and trying to dig deeper into his hero. Unfortunately, Karl, who had first appeared in his previous book, *Silent Tundra*, was living up to his heritage and appeared to be frozen solid beneath the surface.

'Both you and Mrs Frost are booked into the Manchester Royal tonight,' Martine said, breaking his concentration.

'Thanks,' he muttered. 'What?'

Martine looked at him cross-eyed. She slapped a folder onto the desk in front of him. 'Since I'm obviously invisible, I'm going to make myself a cup of coffee. All the info you're not absorbing is in that file. Don't lose it!'

Noah mumbled something out of the side of his mouth that sounded very much like, 'Okay.' Then he ripped a pink Post-it note off his board and replaced it with an orange one from further back in the timeline. The key to Karl's character must be in his past. But where? He looked down on the desk to check his notebook and found it obscured by a file. Where had that come from? He shoved the file in a random drawer.

There was a shuffling noise behind him in the doorway. 'Have you booked the hotel yet?' he asked Martine.

'No.' It was Grace's voice that replied. 'Didn't Martine already take care of that?'

He dropped the stack of Post-it notes and turned round. She looked terrible. As if morning sickness had eaten her up and then spat her out. Her skin was a strange shade of grey and there were large purple bags under her eyes. Although she said the sickness was getting better, she looked so tired.

'How are you feeling?'

'Better,' she said, attempting to sound chirpy and just managing to sound conscious. 'All set for your thing tonight?'

He shook his head. 'No.'

'No, what? I'm not ready? You don't want me to go? Noah, make sense, please.'

She looked so lovely, even pale and washed out. He crossed the room and lifted a hand to stroke her cheek. 'I think you should stay here.'

He'd bought a pregnancy book online and had hidden it inside a folder in his study. Why exactly he'd felt the need to be so anonymous about its purchase and so secretive about its existence, he wasn't sure. He just knew he'd feel embarrassed if Grace found him reading it. She knew all this stuff, had done it all before. He felt such an idiot half of the time, asking stupid questions.

And then he thought that if he didn't sound well-informed, if he didn't keep buying baby stuff, she'd think he wasn't interested. Which he was, on a purely logical level—it was all fascinating. No wonder people called it the miracle of birth. But when he stopped to think that the miracle would be living in his house, that strange feeling happened again. And he didn't like it. It made him feel out of control. Helpless. At the mercy of something greater than himself. So, focusing on the right things to do, the right things to say was better. He could measure his success at that.

If Grace looked pale when he showed her his dinner choices, he knew it was a no-go. In the early weeks he'd known he had to bring her dry wholewheat crackers or plain noodles before ten with a glass of water. Nowadays it could be anything from a list of a dozen weird and wonderful foods. He was busy researching state-of-the-art baby monitors. These were all things he could do without messing up.

Anyway, one of the things he did know from all his reading was that his wife would not survive a journey up the motorway. He shook his head. 'You know I'm right.'

'But why? I'm fine. It was part of our deal, remember? Me going to writing-related events with you.'

Ah, yes. The deal. In which stupid universe had that made sense when he'd thought it up? Certainly not this one. Certainly not now.

A shutter fell over his eyes. She'd do it for him, he knew, even if she felt terrible. But she needed to rest. And he needed twenty-four hours where he didn't feel as if he was trying to be what she wanted and failing her all at the same time.

'You go and lie down. Go back to bed. I'll see you tomorrow lunch time when I get back.'

It was lonely in the manor house that night. Noah's house. Even though she'd been living there for nearly a couple of months, it still felt a bit like a hotel to Grace. Too big. Too smart. Too perfect. It was the house she'd always dreamed of, but it wasn't her home.

Maybe that had more to do with her state of mind—or her state of heart, to be exact—than it did the house. Her first homes with Rob had been small, faceless army quarters, but they'd never seemed that way to her because every one had been filled with happy memories, laughter, passion…

Perhaps that was why Noah's house felt like a show home. Their marriage was legal, of course, but it wasn't real in the sense that her marriage to Rob had been real. She couldn't blame Noah for that. He'd given her exactly what he'd promised her—respect, companionship, more chemistry than she'd expected.

And, in return, she'd foolishly given Noah her heart. It wasn't that he wasn't worthy of it, just that he didn't want it. Try as you might, you just couldn't make someone accept a gift they didn't know existed.

Grace stayed up late, even though it wasn't one of her scheduled nights to chat to Dani and Marissa. It was good to have some time to herself, without her husband in the immediate vicinity, to get some perspective on her situation.

Noah, just like his wayward character, kept himself firmly inside his comfort zone. Oh, not professionally—he was good at pushing the boundaries there—but personally, he was locked up tight. And she knew, just knew, that there was more inside him, that he was selling himself short. But that didn't mean he'd ever let the invisible barrier between them down.

Each sweet gesture, each thoughtful thing he did for her or for their growing baby, rather than filling her with joy, only reminded her that he was always at arm's length, always out of reach. Those things would be lovely if love was the reason behind them, but when that was all there was…

She thought of Rob and how excited he'd been all the way through her pregnancy with Daisy, how he'd kissed her stomach, talked to it, even before the baby could hear. Where Rob had shared himself, Noah brought her things.

She wandered upstairs, barefoot and in her pyjamas, and into the small bedroom they'd discussed turning into a nursery. It was a lovely room, with plenty of space, high ceilings and sash windows. It was all so perfect, but oh-so-empty.

If Noah was incapable of reaching out to her, how would he cope with a child? Would he be as distant with their son or daughter? Her concern turned to anger. It wasn't fair! Her first child had been robbed of a father who'd been devoted to her, and her second child would have a father who was present in body, but…emotionally? Who could tell?

Things had got worse in recent weeks. She had a feeling that Noah knew something was wrong between them but he was running from it. He'd retreated into his book, his fantasy world, rather than face it. Perhaps that was what he always did. Perhaps that was why he'd become a writer in the first place. You couldn't get hurt in a world where you were God and you called the shots, holding everyone's destinies in your hand.

Just once, she'd like to look in his eyes and see the real Noah. She was fed up seeing herself reflected back by the mirror he kept there, the mirror he hid behind.

In the morning Grace rolled over in bed, no Noah to curl up to. She opened her eyes and waited. The urge to be horribly sick was much weaker today. In fact, she was actually very hungry. But working out what she was hungry *for* was another matter.

She scratched the usual suspects—toast, cereal—off her list pretty quick. She wanted something…something salty! Anchovies? No. Not them. Bacon? A shudder ran through her. Bleuch. And then she decided that salty was so last minute and started thinking of spicy things. Chilli sauce? Curry? Ginger-snaps?

Nothing appealed. The only thing she could think of doing was fridge-surfing—sticking her face inside it and seeing what appealed. She lolloped downstairs and into the kitchen and looked at the closed cupboards, hoping for inspiration. Nope.

Noah had a fridge the size of her old bathroom and she yanked the door open as it always seemed to suck itself closed extra hard when she approached it. There, sitting on the middle shelf, with a note propped up against it, was a waxy carton.

Dear Grace,
Thought you might like this for breakfast,
Noah

No love, no kisses, just *Noah*. Before she'd even opened the lid, she knew what it was.

Cold roast pork chow mein.

Her stomach gurgled in anticipation.

See? This was how he broke her heart into tinier and tinier pieces each day. Grace slid onto the floor by the open fridge door and began to cry.

Noah couldn't be doing with all this have-to-be-chauffeur-driven-everywhere-I-go nonsense. He'd taken his car to Manchester, the one admission to his James Bond fixation as a boy. His Aston Martin.

Anyway, motorways were good thinking places. Mile after mile of the same white lines, the same hedgerows and fields, the same crash barriers. The trick was to disengage the creative part of the brain, the right brain, from the driving process and leave it to the left half.

What was he going to do with the troublesome Karl, the spy who refused to love anybody?

Dig deeper. Dig deeper. How do I do that? How do I know if there's anything more inside? I've been digging—mining, even—for weeks and I've come up empty. All I've got is a big hole.

As he drove, Noah rolled Karl's character round in his head, looking at him from every conceivable angle. Eventually, and quite unexpectedly, at Junction Four on the M1, his metaphorical shovel hit something solid. Something resembling a flap or a trapdoor.

He hadn't even begun unpacking when he arrived home. It was mid-afternoon and he found Grace in the garden, staring out across the fields. He walked over to her and kissed her on the cheek. 'How are you doing today?'

He daredn't ask if she'd missed him, just in case she said no.

'Fine,' she said, turning to smile at him, but without using her eyes. 'How was your thing?'

Awful without you beside me. Miserable. It was unbearable not being able to see you, to touch you.

It suddenly hit him that he didn't want to use the smokescreen with Grace any more. He wanted to let her see through it. Great in principle, but the stupid thing had been in place for so many years, he didn't know how to dismantle it.

'Fine,' he finally said. It had been fine. Gone like clockwork. He'd been a roaring success.

That misty look stayed in Grace's eyes all that afternoon, through dinner and into the next week. The only time it faded was when they made love and then she looked as if she was going to cry instead. He wanted to tell her to just let it all out, to drench him with her tears if she wanted, but he didn't know how to make it sound real.

Grace was pulling away. He was losing her.

Maybe she knew. Maybe, without all the picking, she knew. The urge to tell her he'd take the pain away, that it'd be okay, was so strong that he had to bite his tongue. Nice words, but they were a lie. He couldn't tell her that, because he very much feared that everything she was thinking was true.

His brain jumped into action. He had to do something to make her happy.

And he knew just the thing. Her wedding present. A little delayed, to be sure, but she'd understand why when she saw it. It wasn't going to be truly ready for another month, but now was the time to reveal the surprise.

He started making plans immediately and, all the while, his inner Rottweiler was strangely silent.

Noah was behaving most strangely today, Grace thought as she munched her way through a slice of dry toast covered in mango chutney and chocolate sprinkles. He'd been up even earlier than usual. She'd just opened one eye, grunted at the clock and gone back to sleep. But that wasn't all, not by a long shot. After days of scowling at bare patches of wall and muttering to himself, his book filling all his consciousness, suddenly he was back in the real world, smiling, joking and talking.

She had the feeling that this was significant, something important. A turning point.

He bounded into the kitchen and surprised her with a long sweet kiss on the lips, completely ignoring the toast crumbs down her front and the fact that she looked like she'd just escaped from a sci-fi B movie.

'When you've finished that, I think you should get dressed.'

She raised an eyebrow. 'You're getting a bit bossy all of a sudden.'

He tapped his nose. 'You'll see. I've got a surprise for you.'

And then he rushed out of the kitchen again like a mini tornado. Grace put her toast down and smiled. Something was different. He seemed…unguarded, almost open. Her heart quivered at the thought. Was it finally happening? Was he finally ready to stop giving her *things* and give her a piece of himself?

Suddenly, she wasn't hungry any more. Mango chutney and chocolate? Really?

She cleared her breakfast things away and headed upstairs. The morning sickness was definitely fading now she was reaching ten weeks, which was earlier than she'd expected, but a huge relief. And she could get all the way to the top of the staircase at normal speed, without having to lean on the banister for support. Perhaps she was going to start blooming, rather than looking like some weed the dog had dug up.

Jeans and a T-shirt would just have to do, and it was a step up from pyjamas and slobby tracksuits. So much for Noah-the-sexy-author's glamorous wife. When she'd got dressed and run a brush through her hair, she went in search of Noah. She found him in the study, whispering on the phone. He put it down as soon as she crossed the threshold.

'Right. Before we go anywhere, I insist you wear this.' He pulled a woolly scarf out of a drawer and waved it in the air.

'But it's July.'

Noah just grinned. 'Only just. And it's not going round your neck. You need to put it over your eyes.'

His enthusiasm was infectious and she started to laugh. 'Kinky! But…okay.'

He looped the scarf round her head and tied it tight at the back. 'You can save that thought for later, Mrs Frost,' he whispered in her ear. Then he led her out to the car and sat her down in the passenger seat. Her heart started beating fast, partly with nerves, partly with anticipation.

The car journey was not her finest hour, the blindfold making motion sickness a real possibility. Thankfully, the journey was short and it wasn't long before the car stopped and he turned the engine off. Seconds later he opened her door and helped her to stand.

The traffic was loud and she could hear a pedestrian crossing beeping. People were talking and she recognised the sound of shoes on hard ground—on cobbles, if she'd guessed right. They were in the High Street?

'This way…' Noah took hold of her arm under

her elbow and steered her round the car. 'There's a step…and another…' A bell jangled and he guided her through a door. 'Just a bit further…There. You can take off your blindfold now.'

Grace blinked as she pulled the scarf down so it hung loosely round her neck. They were in a shop. She looked round, trying to work out where they were. Dark wood shelves lined the walls. The floor had recently had some very old carpet ripped up because pieces of perished green underlay had collected in the corners. It looked familiar, but…

Suddenly Grace gasped, 'You bought Martin's book shop? Really?'

Noah grinned even wider and nodded. 'I outbid the original buyer, saved it from becoming an extension of Java Express.'

She didn't know what to say. She just left her mouth hanging open and waved her hands around. 'And Martin?'

'Martin is going to run it for me—for the next couple of years, anyway. After that, apparently, Mrs Martin will have my hide. Welcome to Love and Bullets.'

Grace frowned. *'Bullets?'*

'It's going to be a specialist crime and thriller book shop. Shops for niche markets are doing well round here nowadays.'

'And the *love* bit?'

Noah looked a little sheepish. 'Well, in recent

months I realised that not everybody lives on a steady literary diet of blood, espionage and murder, so I made room for a romance section too.'

Grace blinked slowly, thinking that when she opened her eyes again it might all vanish and prove to have been a mirage. 'I think you're barking mad. Wonderful, but barking mad.'

'There's more.'

Grace suddenly felt like sitting down, but there were no chairs so she just leant against an empty shelf. 'More?'

'This way.' He grabbed her hand and pulled her through an archway that was covered in thick plastic sheeting. Grace stumbled through and, when she saw where she was, she said words that her developing baby really ought not to hear.

She was standing in The Coffee Bean, or what once had been The Coffee Bean and was now a completely updated, buffed and polished café. The fantastic Victorian counter had been waxed. It fairly gleamed. The glass had been cleaned and the missing etched panels replaced with good reproductions. And the floor! The broken tiles had been mended. And in the bay window was a vast display case with glass shelves.

Oh, my! What had he done? What had her stupid husband decided to get her now?

Noah had got her a patisserie, that was what. He'd collected all her dreams together and delivered them to her, wrapped in a pink bow. And she hated him for it.

She turned to face him, her hands on her hips. 'When did you buy this?'

The smile slid from Noah's face. 'A few months ago. Java Express had almost sealed the deal, but I went to Caz with a better offer.'

She shook her head, tears filling her eyes. 'Caz let you do this? Why?'

'I…I thought this was what you wanted.'

Grace let out a long sarcastic laugh. 'Why didn't you tell me? Why did you keep all of this a secret from me, Noah?'

The bemused expression he was wearing solidified into irritation. 'It was supposed to be a surprise. Your wedding present. Okay, it's a little late, but I thought you'd understand.'

Anger contorted her features. 'Oh, I understand all right. You can't treat me like one of your characters and plot my life out for me! I'm going to have a baby! How am I going to run a patisserie? Tell me that!'

Noah's forehead creased. 'Babies sleep a lot, don't they?'

Now Grace's laughter became hysterical. 'You have no idea, do you? Absolutely no idea.'

'You don't like it.'

The hormones were ganging up on her again, filling her eyes with tears. Little monsters. 'Noah,' she said in a wavery voice that got quieter and quieter. 'It's beautiful. It's perfect. It's all I ever wanted. But it's just another *thing*.'

He came and stood close to her, face to face. 'And that's wrong?'

Now the tears really fell. 'No. No, it's not wrong. It's just that, when it's the only thing, when there's nothing else…' She gulped in oxygen. 'I can't do this any more. I thought I could, but I can't. I need more.' Her hands wandered to her slightly rounded belly. 'We both do.'

She had to tell him, so she took a really deep breath and drew all her courage into her mouth.

'I…I love you.' If she'd expected some but-I've-always-loved-you-too declaration, like they did in the movies, now was the time. Now was the moment she'd see his face change, his lips move…

He did nothing but take a step backwards and look blankly at her.

'I'm talking about proper love, Noah. To have and to hold love. Yes, we said those words, we said we'd love and cherish, but we didn't mean them that way at the time. But I love you like that now. And I know it's against the rules and not what we agreed, but I can't help it and you can't do anything to change that, even if you want to.'

The pity in his eyes was more than she could handle. 'Grace, I—'

'Don't. Unless you're going to say you feel the same way, just…don't.'

He turned away and walked over to the display cabinet in the window and ran his hands through his hair. 'What do we do now?'

She folded her hands in front of her. 'I'm not going to stop you seeing the baby. In fact, I'll actively encourage it, but…but I don't think I can live with you any more. I don't think I can stay married to you. Not like this. You understand, don't you?'

He stared out of the window and nodded. If she'd have thought him capable of it, she'd have said his heart was breaking. 'I understand.'

It was better this way, it really was. She could raise a child on her own. She'd done it before when she'd been young and clueless, so she could do it again now she was older and clueless. But she couldn't be the mum she needed to be if she spent every day living with Noah, knowing he didn't love her, not even knowing if he *really* wanted this baby.

Suddenly, he spun around to face her and her breath hitched.

'Don't…don't be in a rush, Grace. I don't want to lose you and the baby. We've got that Paris trip, the book launch in a fortnight. Don't go anywhere until after that. Please?'

Oh, yes. The book launch! Better not spoil that.

'If you still feel the same way when we come home, then we'll sit down and talk about it.'

Oh, he was being far too reasonable. She wanted

him to shout, to tell her she was being ridiculous. She'd even settle for relief. Anything would be better than this *non*-reaction. Now was the time to tell him about his stupid spy character, see if she couldn't hit him where it hurt.

'I know what's wrong with Karl.'

He looked momentarily off-balance. 'Huh?'

'Karl. Your super-spy? The reason you can't make him work is *you*.'

'What do you mean?'

She shook her head. Half of her had been hoping he'd tell her not to bother with this now, but he was like a donkey with a carrot dangling in front of his nose.

'I mean, the reason you can't get down to a deeper level with him is because *you* won't go there. Karl is you, Noah. I'm surprised you can't see it. He came out of your subconscious and he's got your weaknesses.'

A look of sudden revelation passed across his face. Good. She hoped something positive would come out of this whole fiasco.

'Until you break through that barrier you use to protect yourself from the world, you are never going to make Karl a convincing hero.'

Grace moved into the spare bedroom that night. Noah tried to insist she stay in the master suite, but she refused, telling him it had never really been her bedroom. She couldn't face rattling round the house knowing Noah was doing the same, so she took herself—and Daisy's laptop—off to bed early. She needed Dani and Marissa more now than ever. When it hit a time that she knew they might be online she sent out a distress call.

Englishcrumpet invites Kangagirl and San-frandani to a private IM conference.
Englishcrumpet: Girls?
Sanfrandani: I'm here!
Englishcrumpet: Oh, Dani! I'm so glad you're there!
Sanfrandani: Let me guess…another Noah-related emergency.
Englishcrumpet: You don't know the half of it! First he blindfolded me and then there was the book shop and then he gave me all my dreams on a plate and I said no and—
Sanfrandani: Grace! Slow down!

Grace make herself breathe deep and slow. Okay, here goes again. Stick to the relevant points. And after she'd filled them in…

Kangagirl: Oh, Grace, I was so sure you two were going to last.
Englishcrumpet: Well, you know what they say about the best laid plans…

Kangagirl: What exactly do they say? Everyone just seems to trail off at that point.
Englishcrumpet: Well, neither do I, actually. What I mean is, it was a bad idea from the start.
Sanfrandani: Are you totally sure there's no way to salvage the marriage?

Grace sat back and stared at the screen for a moment. If Noah could connect with his feelings…If she could accept what he offered and not want more…If she could be sure their child would be brought up in a loving and nurturing environment…

Englishcrumpet: I wish there was. But I really don't think so.

CHAPTER NINE

NOAH stood on the doorstep of Caz's little cottage and rapped on the oversized lion's head knocker. A short time passed and then a voice called, 'It's open!' He pushed the glossy red door and discovered that it swung smoothly, despite its weight.

She was in the kitchen, cooking something odd-smelling. And that wasn't the only thing that was odd. Caz was wearing cowboy boots, a long floaty hippy dress and had a feather stuck in her swept-up hair.

'About time,' was all she said when she saw it was him.

'You know why I'm here, then?'

She nodded and motioned for him to sit down in a sturdy chair next to the bowed pine table. He did as he was told, but had to evict a large ginger cat from the spot first.

The small kitchen was filled with pots, pans, vases. Bits of free-standing furniture and bright hand-painted pottery on the walls. Half-dead herbs hung from an airer hoisted high over his head.

'How can I make her stay?'

Caz stopped stirring what he now thought might be soup and looked at him. 'Noah, you can't make her stay. You have to give her a reason to stay.'

Damn. He was all out of reasons. And, on his own, he wasn't *reason* enough.

'I don't know what to do, Caz. I want her to stay, but I can't give her what she wants. I don't *do* love. Never have. I have no idea how to explain how I feel about her because I don't even know how to define it. Would *you* stay for that?'

She pressed her lips together and thought for a moment.

'Love is more than words, Noah.'

'I know that.'

'Do you?' she said, looking him up and down. 'Really?'

The ginger cat made a reappearance and started rubbing itself on his calf. He tried to shoo it away, not by kicking, more by just nudging with his leg. Caz returned her attention to her soup and, after she'd flung in a few herbs, she nodded to herself, turned down the heat and covered it with a lid. Then she stood with her large bottom cushioning her as she leaned against the kitchen cabinet and folded her arms.

'What's one of the most important things an aspiring writer needs to learn?'

He racked his brain. What had been his weaknesses?

'Spelling?' he said hopefully.

Caz threw her head back and laughed. He'd expected a witch's cackle but it was light and melodious. 'Dig deeper.'

Why was everybody so fixated on digging? It was driving him mad. He was about to ask her as much when one of his hunches hit him and he blurted a phrase out before his conscious brain had even had a chance to give it the once-over.

'Show, don't tell.'

Caz nodded and beamed at him the way a proud teacher would reward her star pupil. 'Exactly. You think about that.'

She turned and put the kettle on and, while she made them both a cup of tea, Noah tried to think about *show, don't tell*. He came up with exactly nothing.

As if she could tell he was struggling, Caz took a different tack.

'Now you're going to be a daddy, you need to think about how a parent loves their child.'

He thought of his parents and also came up blank. Then he thought about Grace and how she would sacrifice everything for Daisy. And, finally, he thought about his own child, the one growing inside Grace, the one he may only get to see on alternate weekends if his wife decided to leave. That pounding, primal, protective thing surged through him again.

Oh.

He looked up at Caz, his mouth open. 'I love that baby already. Even though I haven't met it. Even though I don't know what it will be like.'

She smiled and nodded. 'Of course you do. It won't matter what that child does or says. You will always love it. Always.'

Of course. Unconditional love.

And then another zap hit him. Boy, those hunches were coming thick and fast today.

That was Karl's problem. The girl—the double agent—Karl loves her like that. And he lets her do what she does, even though he knows she'll betray him.

The ginger cat suddenly bounded onto his lap, purred and curled itself up into a ball.

'Yes. That's it,' Caz said. 'Even when it hurts. Even when you lose a little piece of yourself in the loving.'

He understood that much, but…

He looked up at Caz as she peeked into her soup pot. 'But how does this relate to Grace? How can I stop her leaving?'

The feather in her hair fluttered to the floor as she shook her head. 'That's for you to work out. But I'll tell you this…There was a reason I let you buy my coffee shop. And it wasn't so you could hurt Grace.'

* * *

Grace wasn't in when Noah got back that afternoon and he found a note letting him know she'd gone for a walk. She seemed to be doing a lot of that lately. Walking. Leaving the house to get away from him. He chucked his jacket over the back of the sofa and headed for his study.

Once there, he pulled a large pad of paper out of the drawer in his football-pitch-sized desk. It was time to make all these thoughts running round his head physical. Then they couldn't shift and change, one second seeming one thing, the next another. And once he could see his thoughts in stark black ink, maybe he'd be able to make sense of them.

He flipped the pad open and stared at the vast white page. Plain paper had been a deliberate choice—no constricting lines or squares. His thoughts could flow where they needed, unhampered. When he'd finished, the page would be full of scribbled phrases and roughly drawn boxes with arrows sprouting out of them and words. Lots of words. Then he'd sit back and stare at it until he saw the pattern.

But the paper stayed blank. Empty.

Realising that he actually had feelings rather than just instincts had been a major breakthrough for him. But putting those feelings into vowels and consonants was still beyond him. He let out a dry laugh. He made his living creating something out of nothing, with words as his only tool. Why couldn't he turn that skill on himself?

Maybe he could.

Maybe he just needed to take a step back and look at himself as he would one of his characters. Maybe he needed Post-it notes and coloured pens and index cards…He stood up and reached for the shelf that held all his supplies.

No.

That was just time-wasting. Procrastinating. Pen and paper would be enough.

He sat down again and wrote his name in the middle of the white space. Then he underlined it and drew a box round it, waiting for the ideas to start. When they did, he'd hardly be able to scrawl fast enough to keep up, but there was always a moment like this when he sat in the silence and he feared they would never bulge over the lip of his subconscious and begin to flow.

The moment stretched and elongated. Noah's heart began to race. What if they never came, what if—

His pen began to move.

Like he had done with Karl, he started with his past. But, instead of building a history to explain who his character was today, he deconstructed. He pulled the layers away, using his pen as a scalpel, until he could see what had made him this way.

He saw his parents—people who abhorred emotional displays of any kind, who valued stoicism.

And he saw the boy who had tried so desperately to win their approval by squashing himself into that mould, even if it was a painful fit. A boy who grew up to go into the army at nineteen, who literally saw friends die in front of him. A young man who couldn't let himself grieve because, if he'd let it out there and then, he'd have been no use at all to his regiment. So he'd shoved it all in a big hole and built a trapdoor over it.

His hand flew over the paper now, his usually neat writing becoming more angular, less uniform.

He'd carried all of that with him into his post-army life, into his relationship with Sara. Wow. He saw it now. What she'd said. Why she'd left. His glass wall wasn't a barrier keeping him out, stopping him feeling what everybody else felt. It was a shell. A glass shell. His method of self-protection had been the cause of a lot of his unhappiness. It was still causing Grace's.

Grace. How did this all relate to Grace? Because that was what was important now, not his own self-knowledge.

Show, don't tell.

Had his actions communicated more than his words, even his own thoughts?

How had he treated Grace in the last few months? He pushed his pad away and bit the end of his pen. Well, he'd practically manipulated her into marrying him for a start. It hadn't been a conscious plan, but when he looked back on his actions now, it made him uncomfortable. Would she still have married him if she hadn't been backed into a corner? What would she have done if she'd known, at the eleventh hour, he'd decided to try and negotiate for The Coffee Bean? He'd told himself he was doing it for her but, really, he'd done it for himself. Because he wanted Grace to marry him so badly he'd thought he needed a sweetener, something to keep her with him when the honeymoon was over—literally.

And what had he done after she'd pledged to join her life to his? He'd starved her of love and he'd drained her dry.

What else? What else have you done?

He'd tried to be a good husband, the best he knew how to be. It was a pity his knowledge on the subject had been so lacking. He'd only done stupid little things like bringing her dry toast in the mornings when she felt sick, or always making sure he came home with a choice of three different dinners every night. If he'd heard a song on the radio he thought she'd like, he'd bought her the CD.

These were all little things, but in the world of *show, don't tell* they added up to something bigger. Noah's spirits began to lift.

For goodness' sake, he'd bought her a patisserie! Not his brightest idea, it turned out, but you couldn't fault him for trying to give her everything she'd ever dreamed of.

What did all those things say?

He still didn't know. And it was all churning around inside his head, making him feel claustrophobic. He left the study and headed for the garden. As he passed through the kitchen, he was shocked to see it was almost six o'clock and that he'd been holed up in his study for hours.

It was one of those balmy summer evenings that the London suburbs did really well. The horizon was a gentle peach colour and a warm breeze made the trees whisper. His garden was large and rather beautiful, all clipped lawns and leafy trees. No credit to him; he'd inherited them from the previous owner—along with a rather cantankerous gardener who seemed to work different hours every week and had a habit of popping up unexpectedly and scaring the life out of him.

Noah walked across the patio and onto the lawn. There was a beautiful little bench just out of sight, tucked behind a large rhododendron, and he liked to sit there and stare out across the surrounding fields. However, when he got to the spot, he discovered the bench was occupied.

Grace was sitting in one corner. Not sprawled out, relaxing in the early evening sunshine, but hunched into an awkward shape, as if she was trying to physically keep herself together.

In that moment, before she turned and saw him, while a look of unbearable sadness passed across her features, Noah had the strongest hunch of his life. It hit him like an express train going full speed, and he stumbled with the impact of it.

He loved Grace.

With all his heart. With everything he had and everything he was.

That wasn't a hunch, you dummy! It was a feeling. Just like all the other feelings you've been having, but your subconscious dressed them up in disguise and gave them another name so they were safe, so they were acceptable.

And, just like that, the trapdoor sprang open.

Memories and images and everything he'd pressed down and refused to feel for so many years tumbled into his brain. He ignored most of it and rummaged for things labelled *Grace* and *marriage*.

It wasn't just a today thing either, this loving Grace. He'd loved her right from the moment he'd known she was going to be his wife. Maybe even before that. The realisation made him gasp.

Grace, who had apparently been unaware of his presence, jumped up and spun around. 'Noah!'

She was looking at him and he couldn't say a thing. This was the face of the woman he loved. He needed to explore it afresh with his eyes, each familiar curve and line. God, she was beautiful. Of course he'd always thought that, but now…it wasn't just about cheekbones and lashes and lips. It was three-dimensional.

She knew something was different, he could tell. Her eyes held a question. And, since words were still nowhere to be found, he answered it the only way he knew how. He closed the distance between them, pulled her into his arms and kissed her. At first she hesitated, but it wasn't long before the old chemistry started to fizz and she joined him in a deep, hungry, searching kiss.

They made it as far as the conservatory before their patience ran out and the clothes started to come off. A blouse on the wicker chair, a shoe in the kitchen, her skirt left on the stairs, his shirt on the landing…

It was as if he'd been making love in the dark for years and somebody had just turned the light on. No longer was it just about pure physical sensation and muffled feelings he refused to set free.

Afterwards, he lay back and stared at the ceiling. If he'd known it could be like this, that he could feel like this, he'd have started searching for Grace twenty years earlier. Why, oh, why had he wasted all this time?

Even then he couldn't bear any distance between them. He curled round her, dragging her to him, and she intertwined her arms with his and pulled them into her body and kissed his knuckles, his fingers, his palms. At first he was jubilant, ready to leap up and down on the bed and declare his love for her, but then he started wondering why she'd let him make love to her in the first place, why she hadn't shied away from him as she had done in recent days. There had been a poignant sweetness in her lovemaking today, almost a sadness.

As the truth struck home a small pearl of moisture appeared at the corner of his eye. This time together had not been about reconciliation, as he had hoped.

Grace had been saying goodbye.

For the next week, Noah almost buried himself in his study. He didn't know how to fix what had happened between them. He did, however, know how to fix Karl. So he spent his time doing just that. And, as he did, he started to see what Grace had been talking about. He started to see himself, not Karl.

But now Karl loved his double agent girlfriend with true abandon, was willing to die rather than betray her, even if it meant letting her betray him. And, as he wove all of this into the story, the answers started to come to him.

Just telling Grace would not be enough. He was breaking her heart and sounds and syllables would not mend it. Suddenly, he could see so clearly what Caz had been talking about.

The night before they left for Paris, the plan finally clicked into place in his head. He hadn't wanted to jump the gun, to try something and send her running away for ever if he got it wrong, but he was also aware that time was running out and that the hourglass was almost empty.

Paris was just as beautiful. Too beautiful, in fact. Last time she'd been here it had all been new and exciting, her relationship with Noah blossoming. Even she hadn't guessed that in three short months it would all come to an end.

Reminders were everywhere. Places they'd eaten, streets they'd walked down. Noah had even brought them back to the same hotel, although—thank goodness—they occupied a different suite.

Noah was making it hard to let him go.

Harder since they'd made love that day. Every time he looked at her now, her heart did a silly little skip. One better suited to a fourteen-year-old at the beginning of a relationship. It had no place here as they untangled themselves from each other and prepared to go their separate ways.

Grace lay awake in bed early on their second morning there. Her alarm clock showed it was five-thirty but she refused to believe it.

She wished she had Daisy's laptop with her so she could see if Marissa and Dani were online. It would be late in San Francisco, but probably only early evening in Sydney.

Hang on a minute. She could use Noah's laptop.

It was sitting in the lounge of their suite, all set up and ready to go. He'd shown her how to use it weeks ago, scoffing at Daisy's outmoded bit of kit. He'd even offered to buy her a new one, but she'd got used to Daisy's scruffy pink laptop and it felt homely, comfortably shabby in the midst of all Noah's high-tech gadgets.

Noah was breathing softly on his side of the bed. He hadn't even made an attempt to touch her again since they'd last made love. As if he'd silently agreed that they couldn't top what had happened and should leave it as their last sweet memory of the one thing that had always worked in their relationship.

It was almost a relief not to have to wriggle out of his embrace. Almost. She threw the covers back, slid her feet onto the floor and stood up quietly and carefully. Being an early bird, Noah tended to sleep lightly at this time of the morning and it wouldn't take much to rouse him to full consciousness. And she didn't want that. She needed this time on her own.

When she was standing, she crept to the door, walking through the soles of her feet like a dancer. Even she could hardly hear her own footsteps.

Noah's breathing stopped for a moment and she instantly became a statue. But then he started again and he didn't sit up or make any sudden movements, so she finally made it to the door and released the breath that had been trapped in her chest.

* * *

Noah stared at the wall. He'd woken, having heard Grace—no, it was more as if he'd sensed her—creeping out of the room.

Every second of every day she was moving further and further away from him, retreating into herself. He knew he had to put his plan into action soon. But, at the same time, he didn't want to manipulate her. When he asked her to stay it truly had to be her choice and not because he'd carefully and silently removed all her other options.

'Shh!' Grace clapped her hands over the laptop speaker as it merrily chimed, announcing with some self-satisfaction that it was booting up. She glanced at the bedroom door but no light came on and, after a few seconds, she relaxed.

Her fingers rapped out a familiar pattern on the keyboard as she logged onto Blinddatebrides.com, not even having to think about it. She sent out the invitation:

Englishcrumpet invites Kangagirl and San-frandani to a private IM conference.

Nothing happened. Oh, well. She'd known it was a long shot, but she'd been desperately hoping that one of them would be online. She was just about to creep back into the bedroom when the laptop pinged.

Kangagirl: Grace?

Englishcrumpet: Oh, thank goodness! I'm so glad you're here.

Kangagirl: I was just about to leave the office. You just caught me.

Englishcrumpet: Have you got a few minutes?

Kangagirl: Always. Is this a Noah-related emergency?

Englishcrumpet: When isn't it? If I ever get my love life sorted out we'll have nothing left to talk about.

Kangagirl: (grin) We'll just have to start on Dani's, then!

Englishcrumpet: Won't she love that?

Kangagirl: What's up?

Englishcrumpet: I'm regretting saying I'd wait until after the Paris trip to leave. It's just so hard!

Kangagirl: (((hugs))) I'm so sad it didn't work out for you two. I was sure it would.

Englishcrumpet: Me too, or I wouldn't have said yes to him. He's been so quiet the last few days, hardly said a thing to me.

Kangagirl: He's ignoring you?

Englishcrumpet: No. It's not that he's just... not saying much, which is odd in itself.

Kangagirl: Any idea why?

Englishcrumpet: Again, no. And there's this look he gets in his eyes—it's so sad. It makes

my heart break. But I can't stay because of a look. I just feel so guilty.
Kangagirl: You believe you're doing the right thing. I know you do.

Grace stretched her fingers and nodded to herself. Other people might not understand, might say she ought to stick it out for the sake of the baby, but she truly wasn't being selfish. She couldn't bring up a child in that kind of emotional atmosphere. It just wasn't healthy.

Englishcrumpet: I do. I really do. Part of me wishes that Noah would just wake up—

She glanced towards the bedroom door.

Englishcrumpet: Not literally. I mean I wish that he'd make an effort to at least try to change.
Kangagirl: You don't think he will?
Englishcrumpet: I don't think he can. *I'd stay if I thought he would. No. All the silence can only mean one thing—he's given up.*

'Grace?'
On a complete reflex, Grace snapped the laptop closed and jumped away from it. Her heart was pounding so hard it felt as if it would pogo stick right past her throat and out of her mouth.

'Noah! You scared the life out of me!'

No trademark sexy smile. No crinkle round the eyes.

'Sorry.'

She looked at the laptop. 'I was just… chatting to Marissa—you know, the girl in Australia. A wedding crisis or something…'

Why was she lying? This was stupid.

He shrugged. 'You know I don't mind.'

'Thanks.'

'No problem.'

'Well…I'm going for a shower. You carry on.'

But when she opened up the laptop she discovered that closing it had put it on power save and terminated the Internet connection. By the time she'd logged on again, Marissa was nowhere to be found.

It was a couple of hours until breakfast and she and Noah moved around each other like chess pieces, every move designed to keep maximum distance between them. Every move planned ahead.

They didn't bother with room service like last time. Too personal. It was much better in the hotel dining room where they could take comfort from the other people filling up the silences. Where they could breathe out.

'I'll be out all morning,' he told her, even though they'd already discussed it. 'Would you do me a favour?'

'Of course.'

'On the laptop…my book…'

She raised her eyebrows. 'You want me to print it out?'

'No.' He shook his head. 'I think I fixed Karl. I'd be really grateful if you'd read it and tell me what you think.'

'Oh. Okay.'

They were so civilised, weren't they?

He nodded his goodbye and disappeared out of the restaurant.

So civilised it made her want to scream.

Grace didn't feel like sightseeing on her own, so she took Noah's laptop into the terrace café on the roof of the hotel and read his book. At first it seemed to follow the same path, but it was still interesting as, now she had a better idea of the plot, she saw little hints of upcoming problems, had time to appreciate the details.

However, by the time she'd got halfway through she'd forgotten all about being cerebral about it. The plot whizzed along, keeping her hitting the Page Down key pretty quickly, but it was the love story between Karl and Irina that really got her. Where had this come from?

Before, they'd been fine doing all the gun-toting, baddie-busting stuff but, as soon as they'd been alone together they'd gone all two-dimensional. But now…now Noah had a living, breathing love affair on the pages, one that made her gasp and shed a couple of tears.

It was wonderful. The whole book was wonderful.

It was fiendishly clever, exciting, page-turning—all the things he was known for—but it also made her laugh, cry, put her hand over her mouth in horror and snort in anger. In short, it made her *feel*. If this wasn't his biggest selling novel yet, she'd eat his laptop.

She was so proud of him. And when he got back she was going to tell him.

On a whim, she picked up the phone and asked for room service.

The hotel suite door loomed before him. Noah stared at it and stroked the smooth surface of the hotel key card that sat in his pocket. Grace was alone in there. With his book. With Karl and Irina. And if she didn't believe in them, she'd never believe what he had to say. It had been his way of laying the foundations, testing the waters.

He was scared. Good and scared. And it felt good to be scared. His heart tap danced with it. His brain swirled with it. He hated every single sensation, but he welcomed them because he knew what they signalled. He was ready to give Grace what she wanted, what she needed, what she truly deserved. In six months that little baby would be born and he would be the best father in the goddam world, because now he had the tools. He had the heart.

He pulled the key from his pocket and dipped it in the lock.

Grace was waiting for him, sitting on one of the sofas with a chick-lit paperback in her hands. Had she even read his book? Had he left it too late?

She put the book down and stood up. 'Hi.'

'Hi.'

Her face turned a slightly darker shade of pink and she looked at the floor.

'My book—'

'Your book—'

They both spoke at once and then broke off.

'You read it?'

Her face softened and she tipped her head to one side. 'Of course I did. You asked me to.'

Pure Grace. If he'd been thinking straight he'd have known that he didn't need to ask. That was just how she was. Always giving. She was going to be a wonderful mother to their child. Another wave of feeling crashed in, breaking the fear into pieces and tumbling it like pebbles in the surf. He loved her so much. It was time to show her.

It didn't matter what she thought of the book. He was going to tell her anyway.

'Grace, will you come for a walk with me?'

She folded her arms. 'But I…I ordered champagne.' She gestured to an ice bucket on a stand that he could have sworn had just appeared from nowhere. Then she smiled. The first one he'd seen in days. 'To celebrate the book. It really was wonderful—'

He held out his hand. 'Come for a walk. I need to tell you something…show you something.'

She stared at him for a second, her hand half-raised to meet his, half-ready to tuck back into the crook of her opposite elbow.

'Okay.'

CHAPTER TEN

THE sun was behind the high-pitched roof tops, slanting through the gaps between tall houses. Where the light hit the quays flanking the Seine, the pale grey stone was transformed with a golden, rosy glow. Grace and Noah walked through these pockets of light and shade silently, their hands joined, on the surface looking like any other pair of visiting lovers who'd decided to finally emerge from their hotel room.

Noah tried to keep his shoulders loose, his jaw relaxed but, whenever he didn't concentrate on doing just that, the muscles just contracted again. This was it. His moment of truth. He thought he was quite possibly going to die.

They'd started walking near Notre Dame, on the right bank, and now they neared the section near the Louvre.

Grace was staring at the river, steadfastly ignoring the birch trees on the bank—almost as if she couldn't bear to look at them. But he needed her to look at them. He took a deep breath and stopped by the first one.

Gently now. Let it come to her slowly.

'Have you seen all these carvings on the trees?'

She nodded. 'Mmm,' she said in a faraway voice, still watching the waves slap against their stone barriers.

'I would imagine that if someone took the time to leave a message, then the person it was for must mean a great deal to them.'

Now she looked with dull eyes. He stood back. Hoping. Wishing. Praying she'd notice.

Her eyes ran over the bark of the tree and then she sighed and started to turn away. Noah's heart plummeted. But she took one last look and something caught her attention.

'Up there, at the top. What is that?'

He shrugged.

'I didn't notice that before. It's new, carved in a circle round the tree, above all the other messages…'

He followed her eyes, willing her to start reading.

'It's more than just something like *M + D*, isn't it? It's words. It says something.'

Noah held his breath. It said everything.

Grace circled the tree, frowning, then she began to read. '*She is more than her name*— What on earth does that mean? Is that supposed to be romantic?'

He didn't say anything, just put his hands in his

pockets and started walking towards the next tree, hoping she'd take the hint. She did. But she kept frowning and looking back at the first tree. His poor quivering heart began to steady itself.

They reached the next one and, just as he'd known she would, she stopped and inspected this one without any prompting.

'There's more…listen! *Free and unearned favour.* This just gets weirder and weirder.'

Now she walked more quickly to the next tree, he walked behind her, trying to regulate his breathing.

'And, despite my current fame…'

She ran back to him, her eyes now bright and alert, totally caught up in the puzzle.

'Noah, it's…Wait. I've just got to—'

She didn't finish her sentence, but ran back to the first tree, circled it, ran to the second, did the same…

'It's a poem!' she said when she'd joined him again. 'Come on. There must be more.'

Good. She liked the poem. Well, a sonnet—of sorts. Clumsy and inelegant by Shakespeare's standards, but he had it on good authority that it came straight from the author's heart, and that had to count for something, didn't it? Finally, he'd come up with a way of *showing* her. Caz had been right. Love was more than words, but words were the best tool at his disposal, so he'd hoped he'd found a way to make them count.

He caught her up at the next tree.

'Read it,' she said, smiling.

He didn't need to look at the scratchings in the bark. In the last few days, while Grace had been sleeping heavily, he'd spent the few hours before dawn shaping them into what he wanted to say. But he played along with her. For now.

He took a deep breath. *'I am humbled to have known her.'* The words sounded strange in his ears. He'd never said them out loud before and it was a bit like going out in public in just his underwear.

Grace sighed. 'It's so beautiful. I wonder if there will be a name at the end, a clue to who wrote it.'

He shrugged again. No. No name. Not his, anyway. But there was a clue.

He was scared of the clue.

Once she'd read it, his life would split in one of two ways—one heaven, one hell. And only she could decide.

She jogged from tree to tree, calling out the lines, chattering about what it meant, pondering the mystery. Noah tried to keep his façade calm and collected, but it was difficult without his glass shell. Everything kept floating to the surface and he had to shove it down again, saying, *Wait. Not yet.*

Three more trees to go. Was it possible for a man of his age and build to just pass out? Grace came back and grabbed his hand, dragging him on.

'*Joined with me, she makes my soul complete.* Only two more trees now. This must be near the end!'

Oh, that her smile would stay, that the joy in her eyes would not flicker out when she reached the last tree.

'*And I will die if I cannot always look upon her face.*' Tears sprang to her eyes and she clapped a hand to her chest. 'Oh, my word…'

No. His words. His heart. For her to accept or reject.

Before she reached the last tree, Noah let go of her hand and stopped as she ran ahead, his heart pounding so loudly in his ears that he could no longer hear the river. She circled the last silver birch in the row. This time, her mouth moved but no sound came out.

She looked at him and he thought he would melt away into nothing.

He walked towards her and, without looking at the tree, completed the sonnet. 'She is my love, my heart…' here his voice thickened so much it cracked '…my only Grace.'

So many emotions flickered over her face, he didn't have time to read them. She marched back to him and grabbed his upper arms, her fingers shaking as they dug into his muscles.

'Why?' she said, almost angry. 'Why did you write that?'

Then the fierceness evaporated and she looked into his eyes. He looked straight into hers. Confusion, hope, fear and desperation all swirled and mingled there. It was as if he were looking right into her heart. He did his best to drop his own shutters and let her see his. Her eyes flicked rapidly right to left as if she were trying to read him, as if she was scared of what he might be saying. And then the tears fell, her mouth crumpled. She nodded.

He kept looking into her eyes and freed his arms so he could touch her face, wipe her tears with the pads of his thumbs. And then he lowered his lips to hers and the kiss they shared was hot and sweet and perfect. It wasn't just their lips meeting, fusing. Something happened—a new feeling he'd never experienced before and suspected he never would again. It was as if, in the back of his head, he heard a clunk, a click, and everything in the world slotted into its right place. He and Grace might have been married for three months, but now they were joined.

'I love you,' he whispered against her lips, and she just began to cry again.

The only thing better than a honeymoon in Paris was a second honeymoon in Paris, Grace decided as she lay in Noah's arms the day after they returned from their extended trip. It had been fabulous. Even better than the first one. And not many women got to boast about two honeymoons in Paris within a few months. And with such a man. She sighed and looked at him. He'd changed so much and she was horribly proud of him. She had no doubt now that he would be a wonderful father.

He was her soulmate. He was a different fit to Rob, but still it worked. She didn't understand how there could be two people who could match her so completely, especially when they were two very different men. But then love wasn't static. It could cope, she reckoned.

It was six o'clock and she was wide awake. Unusually for Noah, he was not. Thankfully, the morning sickness was much improved and she was happy lying in bed watching Noah breathe and feeling the weight of the arm draped across her midriff. She knew she shouldn't, but she couldn't help trailing her fingers across his arm, feeling the soft hair there.

Suddenly, he sniffed and twitched. He opened his eyes, dozy and unfocused at first, but then he saw her and a huge sexy smile broke across his face.

'Good morning, Mrs Frost.'

She smiled back. 'Good morning, Mr Frost.'

Then he dived under the sheet and kissed the slight round of her tummy. 'Good morning, Little Frost.' Then he reappeared and kissed her on the nose. 'I love you, Grace.'

'I love you too, Noah. My Noah.' She ran her fingers through his hair as she gave him an indulgent look. 'You must have said that a thousand times in the last week. I get it now. You can stop if you like.'

He looked wounded. 'Never! If I only say it nine hundred and ninety-nine times in the next week, you have permission to slap me.'

'I'll keep count,' she said, giggling.

'You'd better.'

They dragged themselves out of bed and down into the kitchen. Grace had a yearning for a full English breakfast now the morning sickness seemed to have waned almost completely. And, as Noah cooked, they discussed the future of the book shop with its attached patisserie, an easy flow from one to the other. If she hadn't been so angry the first time she'd seen it, she'd have realised what a wonderful idea it was.

Grace jumped up to sit on the counter and watched Noah fry her eggs. 'Daisy is thrilled at the idea of helping out while she studies and Caz has been moaning she needs something to keep her occupied. She also felt really bad about laying off all the old Coffee Bean staff and she's begging me to consider re-hiring them. Between all of us, I reckon we can make it work.'

Later that morning the doorbell rang and Noah answered it, then returned to the kitchen, where Grace was sitting, with a small square package in his hand.

'What's that?' she asked and walked over to look at it.

'Don't know.' He turned it over and read the

return address. 'It's addressed to me from an Internet company based in Devon. Ceramics or something.' He shook his head.

'It's not *another* thing for the baby, is it?'

Noah had been filling the nursery with books and toys and all sorts of strange gadgets with alarming speed. She really must encourage him to get on with the third draft of his book. That would keep him out of trouble and curb the Internet shopping spree.

'No. Or nothing I've bought.'

She narrowed her eyes, but he stared back at her, the picture of innocence.

'We'll see,' she said, holding out her hand. He gave the package to her and she peeled back the parcel tape and looked inside. Something—an irregular something—was rolled in bubble wrap. And there was a piece of paper. She put the box on the kitchen table and pulled the scrap out.

'It's a message from…Daisy,' she said, one eyebrow shooting heavenwards. 'It's definitely for you. Listen…

Dear Noah, here's a little gift to say thanks, I'm happy I picked you, and I'm glad you've joined our family.'

She passed the scrap of printed paper to Noah, who examined it.

'It's just a short message she must have typed in on the website when she ordered the…whatever it is.'

'I think you'd better open it.'

Noah shrugged and pulled the box across the table to him. Then he removed the *thing* and started to unwrap it. As he revealed what it was, Grace began to laugh uncontrollably. 'Oh, that girl! She's priceless!'

It was so funny. Noah was just staring at it, completely lost for words.

It was an electric-blue mug with the words 'Hot Papa' written on it in navy glitter. She took it from him and placed it on the shelf next to her pink mug.

Finally, Noah began to chuckle. 'A matching pair. But…*Hot Papa*?'

Grace walked over to him and looped her arms around his neck. 'She's not wrong, you know,' she said. And then she drew him into a lingering kiss and let him show her just how right his stepdaughter had been.

EPILOGUE

Private IM conference between Kangagirl and Sanfrandani:

Kangagirl: I knew it! I told you right from the start that Grace and Noah were going to end up together, didn't I?
Sanfrandani: Yes, Marissa. You did.
Kangagirl: I've got a sixth sense about these things.
Sanfrandani: Of course you have.
Kangagirl: I have! And you know what, Dani?
Sanfrandani: Uh-oh.
Kangagirl: My 'sense' tells me you're next.
Sanfrandani: LOL!!!! That's so funny, Marissa.
Kangagirl: You'll see.
Sanfrandani: No way. And, Marissa?

Kangagirl: Yes?
Sanfrandani: Wipe that goofy smile off your face!
Kangagirl: !!!!!!!!!!!

* * * * *

*In honor of our 60th anniversary,
Harlequin® American Romance® is celebrating
by featuring an all-American male each month,
all year long with*
MEN MADE IN AMERICA!
*This June, we'll be featuring American men
living in the West.*

Here's a sneak preview of
THE CHIEF RANGER *by Rebecca Winters.*

*Chief Ranger Vance Rossiter has to confront
the sister of a man who died while
under Vance's watch…
and also confront his attraction to her.*

"Chief Ranger Rossiter?" The sight of the woman who'd stepped inside Vance's office brought him to his feet. "I'm Rachel Darrow. Your secretary said I should come right in."

"Please," he said, walking around his desk to shake her hand. At a glance he estimated she was in her midtwenties. Her feminine curves did wonders for the pale blue T-shirt and jeans she was wearing. "Ranger Jarvis informed me there's a young boy with you."

The unfriendly expression in her beautiful green eyes caught him off guard. "Yes," was her clipped reply. "When we arrived in Yosemite the ranger told me I couldn't go anywhere in the park until I talked to you first."

"That's right."

"Knowing you wanted this meeting to be private, he offered to show my nephew around Headquarters."

So this woman was the victim's sister…. "What's his name?"

"Nicky."

The boy who haunted Vance's dreams now had a name. "How old is he?"

"He turned six three weeks ago. Were you the man in charge when my brother and sister-in-law were killed?"

"Yes. To tell you I'm sorry for what happened couldn't begin to convey my feelings."

The woman's gaze didn't flicker. "I won't even try to describe mine. Just tell me one thing. Was their accident preventable?"

"Yes," he answered without hesitation.

"In other words, the people working under you fell asleep on your watch and two lives were snuffed out as a result."

Hearing it put like that, he had to set the record straight. "My staff had nothing to do with it. I, myself, could have prevented the loss of life."

Ms. Darrow's expression hardened. "So you admit culpability."

"Yes. I take full blame."

A look of pain crossed over her features. "You can just stand there and admit it?" Her cry echoed that of his own tortured soul.

"Yes." He sucked in his breath.

"I work for a cruise line. Aboard ship, it's the captain's responsibility to maintain rigid safety regulations. If a disaster like that had happened while he was in charge he would have been relieved of his command and never given another ship again."

Rachel Darrow couldn't know she was preaching to the converted. "If you've come to the park with the intention of bringing a lawsuit against me for negligence, maybe you should." It would only be what he deserved.

"Maybe I will."

In the next instant, she wheeled around and hurried out of his office. Vance could have gone after her, but it would cause a scene, something he was loath to do for a variety of reasons. In the first place, he needed to cool down before he approached her again.

The discovery of the Darrows' frozen bodies had affected every ranger in the park. A little boy had been orphaned—a boy whose aunt was all he had left.

* * * * *

Will Rachel allow Vance to explain—
and will she let him into her heart?
Find out in
THE CHIEF RANGER
Available June 2009
from Harlequin® American Romance®.

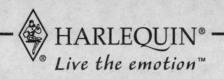

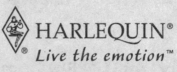

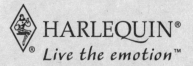

HARLEQUIN®
INTRIGUE®

BREATHTAKING ROMANTIC SUSPENSE

Shared dangers and passions lead to electrifying
romance and heart-stopping suspense!

Every month, you'll meet six new heroes
who are guaranteed to make your spine tingle
and your pulse pound. With them you'll enter
into the exciting world of Harlequin Intrigue—
where your life is on the line
and so is your heart!

THAT'S INTRIGUE—
ROMANTIC SUSPENSE
AT ITS BEST!

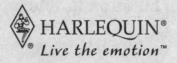

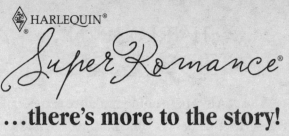

HARLEQUIN®
Super Romance®

...there's more to the story!

Superromance.
A *big* satisfying read about unforgettable
characters. Each month we offer *six* very different
stories that range from family drama to adventure
and mystery, from highly emotional stories to
romantic comedies—and much more! Stories
about people you'll believe in and care about.
Stories too compelling to put down....

Our authors are among today's *best* romance
writers. You'll find familiar names and talented
newcomers. Many of them are award winners—
and you'll see why!

If you want the biggest and best
in romance fiction, you'll get it
from Superromance!

Exciting, Emotional, Unexpected...

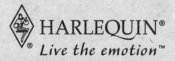

HARLEQUIN®
Live the emotion™

HARLEQUIN®
Presents

The world's bestselling romance series...
The series that brings you your favorite authors,
month after month:

Helen Bianchin...Emma Darcy
Lynne Graham...Penny Jordan
Miranda Lee...Sandra Marton
Anne Mather...Carole Mortimer
Melanie Milburne...Michelle Reid

and many more talented authors!

Wealthy, powerful, gorgeous men...
Women who have feelings just like your own...
The stories you love, set in exotic, glamorous locations...

HARLEQUIN®
Presents

Seduction and Passion Guaranteed!

HPDIR08

Harlequin® Historical
Historical Romantic Adventure!

*Imagine a time of chivalrous
knights and unconventional ladies,
roguish rakes and impetuous
heiresses, rugged cowboys
and spirited frontierswomen—
these rich and vivid tales will
capture your imagination!*

*Harlequin Historical . . .
they're too good to miss!*

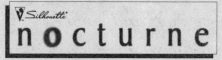

SPECIAL EDITION™

Emotional, compelling stories that capture the intensity of living, loving and creating a family in today's world.

Desire

Modern, passionate reads that are powerful and provocative.

nocturne

Dramatic and sensual tales of paranormal romance.

Romantic SUSPENSE

Romances that are sparked by danger and fueled by passion.